APOLLO'S GIFT

A Fantasy Romance

By
Sandy L. Rowland

Apollo's Gift © 2013 Sandy L. Rowland
All rights reserved

License Notes

This book is a work of fiction. The names, characters, places, businesses, and incidents are products of the writer's imagination or have been used fictitiously and are not to be construed as real. Any resemblance to persons, living or dead, actual events, locales or organizations is entirely coincidental.

Cover Design © Kelli Ann Morgan
Inspire Creative Services
www.inspirecreativeservices.com

Interior book design by
Bob Houston eBook Formatting
http://about.me/BobHouston

ISBN: 978-0-9858518-3-5

Books by Sandy L. Rowland

APOLLO'S GIFT

CONQUERED

DEDICATION

To my husband Rob, who continues to
make love real.

APOLLO'S GIFT

Sandy L. Rowland

CHAPTER ONE

Something drew Cassie Priam to Delphi.

She trudged the path, her hiking boots crunching with each step. The fragrance of cypress, wild flowers and sun-baked earth brought visions to her mind of another time. Ancient Greece, when seekers of knowledge had climbed Mount Parnassus to bring gifts to the oracle, and gain wisdom. Cassie had dreamed of the path she now trod, but those night visions centered in a time three thousand years ago when Apollo had ruled the spot.

The summer-blue sky welcomed her. Cassie stopped to adjust her wide-brimmed hat, opened her bottle of water and gulped. The cool liquid splashed over her lips, leaving drops, trickling down her neck and between her breasts. The temple wasn't much farther. Odd, but she'd known the place before ever setting foot amid the columns, as if she belonged there.

She'd always had an interest in Greek myth, but these last months bordered on obsession. This trip was supposed to get her mind off her last break-up. It had shaken her. Friends insisted she join them for a summer in Europe, gain a new perspective, maybe have a fling with some hot Italian or Greek. Yeah, like that was going to happen. She'd shared a few meals with a nice guy called George, but it was too soon to risk her heart. While her friends had enjoyed the nightlife, she'd huddled in her hotel room and read Homer. No wonder guys dumped her. She was a math major for hell's sake and didn't have a romantic bone in her body, much less an adventurous spirit.

Her friends were still sleeping off their dancing and wine when she'd left early this morning. Tonight she'd fly home to Washington. Back to her well ordered and predictable life of logic and reason. She'd welcome it after this bizarre fixation with Delphi.

Turning off the Via Sacra path, she entered the site. Stone lined the area, half tumbled and decayed. The foundation remained a footprint. When she closed her eyes she could imagine the grandeur of perfectly chiseled pillars towering above her. And envision the carefully guarded crevice, the world's navel, where the oracle had raved her prophecies.

Sun heated her khaki shorts and lemon yellow t-shirt until sweat dampened them both. Cassie pulled off her hat, fanned herself with it and moved into the protective shade of a secluded cypress tree. She sat on the ground amid the weeds and leaned back against a rock slab of decaying wall. Summer warmth leached from the stone into her bones. Staying up late reading and waking early to make her trek added to heat-induced drowsiness. She just needed a quick close of her eyes.

* * *

Cassie squinted against harsh light. "It's that dream again," she grumbled. She shielded her eyes from the glare with her hand. Her vision adjusted. Sure enough, she sat in the rough robe of a priestess amid pristine columns of Delphi in its prime. Even her dreams were dull. Babbling nonsense over a pit. How silly was that?

"Cassandra," said a male voice loaded with seductive timbre.

She shifted her gaze in the direction of the voice and locked onto an incredibly handsome man standing beside a pillar. A mane of golden waves topped with a laurel wreath crowned his classic features, and accentuated eyes as blue as the Mediterranean set against a golden tan. "I've been waiting for you."

Blinking, she focused on the exquisite masculine form. Not a statue, but worthy of marble. This was an interesting change. "Um, you must have me mixed up with someone else." The man had to be a god. No mortal looked that good. This dream was looking up. She shifted her toga and got to her feet.

He smiled, the kind that movie stars flashed

and weakened more than a girl's knees. "There's no mistake. I've brought you a gift."

He strode toward her, his muscles rippling with fluid movement. The man was beyond beautiful. She didn't bother asking how he knew her name. It was a dream and the rules of logic held no sway here. But after being dumped by the last guy, she was cautious of a tryst, even with a vision. "I'm not who you're looking for." She twisted her linen garment in her fingers.

He closed the distance between them. Even in the day's heat, she felt warmer with him near. His mouth tightened. "You're my Cassandra."

"Your Cassandra?" She'd just read the story of the Trojan War again last night. Her stomach plummeted. If her dream cast her as Cassandra ancient prophetess of Troy, then this hot specimen had to be..."Apollo?"

"Yes." His gaze pierced through her like twin beams of cobalt light.

"Of course!" Standing in the presence of a god should have terrified her, but it didn't. This was only a dream, making conversation with deity no big deal. Maybe he came from a bit of over-ripe goat cheese she'd eaten earlier.

"You remember me?"

"Not really, but you do seem familiar."

His full lips tightened into a firm line. "I am Phoebus Apollo. Son of Zeus. God of light and prophecy, among other things."

"You're fantastic, so imperious and arrogant.

Much better than I'd imagined."

"Imagined?" His eyes narrowed.

"Yes. You're better looking and have such a commanding presence." The dream Apollo didn't appear to enjoy her compliment. Sparks shot from his eyes and it creeped her out.

"I *am* Apollo." The ground quaked, knocking her to the earth. "And you are Cassandra, my priestess, Oracle of Delphi and my consort."

The ground continued to shake. The man's body lifted four feet above her and hovered, glowing like a lit candle. Her heart slammed against her ribs. She tucked her head and curled into a fetal pose, trembling. Cassie awaited the god's wrath. If she died in her dream, would she expire in real life?

The shaking stopped. She waited, but nothing happened.

Cassie opened her eyes to slits. She hadn't been annihilated. No thunderbolts streaked across the sky, and no fissure gaped to swallow her whole. Tremors had put her off balance, but they weren't worthy of panic. *Get hold of yourself.* This was only a dream. Any minute she'd wake. And since this was her dream, she refused to cower. Lifting her head. Why not enjoy it and have a little fun? "Great Apollo, what is your will?" She did her best to sound serious and sat back on her heels.

He floated like a cloud. "I've come to give you a gift."

"Beware of Greeks bearing gifts," she murmured. "Thank you for the offer, but I couldn't possibly accept."

"It is my will." Another tremor sent her to all fours and her hand struck rough stone.

"Fine." She shifted to her bottom and rubbed a red patch on her palm. "What is it?"

He landed beside her, his white robes fluttering in the breeze. "The greatest of all gifts, prophecy."

She got to her feet and glared at the dream masquerading as Apollo. His warm breath grazed her cheek. "Oh, no," she argued. "That never turns out well."

"I admit that in your previous incarnation things didn't go as I'd planned." He shrugged one shoulder. "But I've negotiated with Hades, and paid a high price so your soul could take form in this body." He leaned over her. "You're my Cassandra, Princess of Troy."

"Whoa! You bought my soul?" She backed up into a marble wall. "Even if I believed I had one, I'm sure it would belong to me. Who said you could buy it?" This was a nightmare. "And this whole prophecy deal, that was a disaster. Apollo gave Cassandra that gift and then cursed her so no one believed her warnings. I think I'll pass."

"No, faithless, mortal woman. The curse came by way of your lie. You promised me your virtue and then spurned me." His honeyed voice had taken on a definite edge.

"Hey, not me." She threw her hands up in defense. "Cassandra was murdered ages ago and my *virtue* is not open to discussion. I don't even believe in gods and prophecy." *Wake up, Cassie. Wake up.*

"Hear me." He stroked her hair with the tips of his fingers sending a tingle over her scalp. She wanted to move away but couldn't, his soft, seductive tone freezing her in place. "You have a chance to make amends and give yourself to me. Honor your promise and all will be well."

"For who?" Even for a dream, this was a pretty lame line.

The corners of his mouth twitched. "You are still pure."

"Well, that's none of your business." Heat rushed into her face. She brushed the dirt from her robe and glanced at him from the corner of her eye.

"I am a god and discern that you haven't known a man." A satisfied smile spread across his full, perfect lips. "I am pleased."

"Right," she grumbled. The man was exasperating.

"You doubt me."

This had gone on too long. "Enough already. You're part of a dream brought on by hot sun and a romantic location, nothing to take seriously."

At least six foot five, he towered over her like an ionic column. He moved closer, pressing her against the wall. Her heart thumped in response.

He's a dream, a deliciously tempting dream.

He leaned in, his mouth a kiss away. His breath tantalized with the scent of nectar. "I'm real and eternally serious."

She licked her dry lips. Maybe she was wrong and this wasn't a nightmare but a really, really good dream.

"This is no dream." He brushed his lips over hers, soft, warm and as addictive as the fabled ambrosia. She leaned in wanting more, but he denied her. "It's done."

"What's done?" she murmured.

"The gift is given."

"No. Wait."

"Once given, I can't take it back."

Panic tightened her chest. *It's a dream. Damn it.* "Take it back." She sputtered and spit. Something had to rid her of his gift. "I won't use it. Prophecy or not, nothing can make me tell people." She wiped her wet mouth on her sleeve.

A beautifully irritating smile spread over his mouth. "Ah, Cassandra, you haven't changed. The same argument you tried in your last incarnation. I've missed this."

"Ugh." She stomped her foot. "This is my dream. I'm in control and I refuse."

He tilted his golden head and studied her. "I think not. It's against your nature to leave thousands to die when you have the ability to warn them."

She squared her shoulders. "This is not the

city of Troy and I'm not your dead princess. Even if this gift were real, which it's not, no one would listen to me. People don't believe in prophecy these days. I don't even believe in it. They'll shoot me full of meds and lock me in a rubber room."

His eyes softened. "Millions will suffer if you don't try."

"Millions?" Definitely a nightmare.

* * *

Cassie jolted awake. Her palms were damp, her heart pounding. What a nightmare. She rubbed her mouth with the back of her hand, hoping to remove the memory. She shuddered. It was only a dream. It had to be. Gods didn't exist; neither did divine gifts and curses. She followed her urge to spit away what clung to her lips, but the slight pressure of a kiss remained.

The sun remained high in the sky. She couldn't have slept for more than a few minutes. "Apollo, really," she muttered. It would figure that the hottest guy she'd ever met would be an annoying figment of her creative mind. "Men are jerks." She shook her head and her gaze fell to her hat lying beside her, a wreath of laurel laid over the wide brim.

"Damn."

CHAPTER TWO

"So beautiful." Apollo watched unseen as Cassandra stepped into the steamy shower. Travertine tiles lined the walls, but it wasn't the stone he focused on, it was the woman. He'd had many lovers, but this ebony-haired beauty had weighed on his mind for the last three thousand years. Was it her soft curves, long legs and violet eyes that captivated him or her inner fire?

Cassie turned to face him and threw her head back, water pouring over her dark tresses, molding them against her shoulders and around her ample breasts like fingers holding ripe pomegranates. He hungered to taste that fruit. Indulging in the temptations of the flesh no longer dishonored a mortal father or a woman's position. And this mortal woman tempted him. Beads of moisture ran over her satin skin and dripped from her rosebud nipples, calling him to suckle at her warmth, and then lower to that temple created by the gods, where he would worship for long, blissful hours.

But he wouldn't compel her. It was within his

power to act as Zeus often had, and transform into a shower of gold or rays of welcoming light, cover her innocence and know her. Take her. Apollo shook his head. He'd changed, grown perhaps, if it were possible for the gods to become more. He desired more than Cassandra's body, he wanted her eyes to sparkle at his approach, and her heart to leap with joy at his touch. He wanted her love. Artemis might be right; he thrived on competition and a challenge. Gaining Cassandra's love was a challenge. Cassie had spurned him ages ago and he hadn't taken it well.

Not this time. He had a plan.

She dried herself with a pink towel and rubbed almond-scented lotion over her delectable curves. How he longed to be that lotion and glide against her skin. He breathed in and released it slowly. Or taste it, licking up the sweet oil for the promise of something sweeter, Cassandra. He groaned within. The wager demanded that he wait. He refused to leave her virtue and safety to chance. He'd watched over her since birth and, seen or unseen, he'd stay by her side. Even if it tried him. Like this moment. This time he'd handle it differently. Rather than trading the gift of prophecy for pleasures of her flesh, he'd given the gift to tie her to him. Cassandra had no idea of his true intentions. How could a mortal understand the mind of a god? Once she called upon him for aid, and knew his heart, she'd willingly consent to his will. But her consent wasn't enough; he demanded her passion and her love. He'd woo her in her dreams and bring her warnings as she slept. The maniacal ravings of ancient times would be a cruel punishment in this world.

Humanity lacked faith. They no longer prayed to the gods or valued their wisdom, but looked to small oracles they held in their hands to gain knowledge, phones, pads and computers had replaced Delphi and Olympus. Foolish mortals. The gods existed and it was time humanity remembered.

He'd gifted her with prophecy, now to point her in a direction to use it. *Something small to start*....Apollo lost his thought as Cassandra bent over to retrieve a towel from the floor. Perfectly rounded hips set upon shapely legs met his hungry gaze. The woman tried him and she didn't know it. His fingers itched to caress those mounds and pull her against himself. One day soon, after she valued the gift, knew it's importance, and her desire matched his own, then he'd have her. Not before.

* * *

Cassie's mother eyed her over a cup of black coffee at breakfast. Her raven hair was cut short to control the riot of curls threatening her sleek look of flawless skin and navy suit. "It's for the best. Your father and I agree that living at home while you attend school will bring much-needed opportunity. You only met rabble and brought home poverty-stricken students when you lived in the dorms. We want more for you." She scraped butter from her toast and nibbled a dry corner.

"I appreciate the thought, but I liked those people. They were real." Cassie shoveled blueberries into her mouth and chewed.

"Real? Planning for your future, that's real. Spending your time working out equations and avoiding social activities, it's just not right. What kind of life is that for a beautiful young woman? It's just not..." Her mother pursed her lips. "You need situations where you can meet the right people."

Cassie breathed in and out through her nose as she finished chewing and silently counted to ten. By *right* people, her mother meant wealthy young men with bright futures and the appropriate family connections. Cassie didn't care for any of it. She'd dated enough of those men and they'd all walked away from her. She'd resigned herself to the fact that they didn't want her. Why torture herself? Numbers didn't judge, and she preferred their silent acceptance and calculated outcome to romantic failure. "I have plans for my life. I want to..." Her mother's phone vibrated and hummed beside her plate.

"Excuse me, I have to take this. It's my office."

"Oh yes, your office." Cassie felt the familiar frustration rise inside. *Big emergency. Maybe another debutant had a pimple.* Practicing dermatology mattered to her mother, not that she didn't love

Cassie, but her mom just couldn't focus on more than one thing at a time. For now, medicine won out.

While her mother finished the call, Cassie mused over her options. Play the part of the dutiful daughter and put up with her parents interference, or what? She pushed a lone blueberry around her bowl with her spoon. The last orb stubbornly avoided direction, running ahead and then escaping. *Like me.* That's what her parents saw in her, a young woman in need of shepherding into an appropriate life. Cassie set down the spoon and glared at the berry. *Fine.* She might live at home while attending school, but that's as far as she'd go. No setting her up with the "right" men.

"Good morning, princess." Her dad had called her princess for as long as she could remember but, since her disturbing dream at Delphi, the endearment prickled her skin. *It was only a dream. Get over it.*

"Morning." Cassie forced her mouth into a weak smile.

Her dad took a seat beside her at the gleaming cherry-wood table, poured cream into his coffee and stirred. That glazed look covered his eyes, the one that meant trouble he couldn't discuss. "What?" he murmured, and stirred, the spoon clinking against bone china.

"Dad." Cassie touched his hand, hoping to bring him back from some dark precipice shadowed in his hazel eyes. Things must be rough at the Pentagon. "Well, this should make you happy, I'm living here while getting my masters."

He shifted his gaze, landing on her face and smiled. "I'm glad. We haven't seen you all summer and I've missed you."

"You won't see me much. I'll be busy with school and you're schedule is crazy."

"Being secretary of state is demanding, but I'll make time."

She saw truth shining in his eyes and it warmed her. His brow furrowed. "And don't forget your mother, with all the volatile news coming out of the Middle East, she was a nervous wreck while you were gone. I had to talk her out of insisting you cut your trip short."

Cassie glanced at her mother gesturing as she spoke on the phone, surprised she worried over much, except her patient's acne. "Well, there's nothing volatile about me or Georgetown. We're as dependable as a quadratic equation."

He winked. "Nothing wrong with that. Keep your feet on the ground and your head on the facts and you'll always know what course to take." He stood and pressed a kiss to the top of her dark hair, signaling the end of the discussion. "Living here is the logical answer and will move your life forward. You'll see."

She tilted her head up and stared at him. He'd aged. His dark brown hair grayed to salt and pepper. Creases deepened around his mouth and etched worry into his brow. How had she missed the change in him? Her heart softened. "Okay, Dad."

CHAPTER THREE

"Order and logic...yeah right," Cassie muttered, and shifted her feet. The morning line at Starbucks on campus snaked around tables to the door. It was her second day and, so far, she had a handle on her program, but not her dreams. Apollo invaded her sleep, plying her with wine and poetry in an effort to seduce. Damn, he was good at it. Unfortunately, that wasn't the entire dream. It always evolved into reliving the destruction of Troy with her playing the part of the doomed prophetess. Yeah, not getting much sleep—and she felt it.

The line inched forward, some people making multiple orders. Cassie shrugged her shoulders trying to loosen the confining charcoal suit. Mother had insisted she wear professional dress and dragged her reluctant body to stores for clothes and shoes, all tight, none her style and definitely not comfortable. Cassie preferred something loose and loaded with pockets.

Another step toward the counter. *At this rate, I'll be twenty minutes older before I reach the front. All for coffee, sinfully addictive coffee.* Another step. Her mind wandered to other sinful pleasures, dreams of the Greek god. Ugh. She had to stop it. She was hung up on a dream.

He'd played the lyre last night and sung the verse he'd composed—Ode To Cassandra he'd called it. Heat flooded her cheeks. Where had she gotten such a lusty imagination? And why dreams of Apollo? Why not someone real, like that cute guy with the buzzcut and sexy leather jacket she'd spied every morning? She craned her neck, hoping to find him ahead in line. Her perusal met with shades of sweatshirts and jeans, but no leather capped with a chocolate buzz. She let out a breath of frustration.

"Hello," the voice rumbled behind and to her left.

She turned and met dark eyes of burnt umber and a dazzling smile. Mr. Buzzcut looked even more interesting up close. "Hi. Here to get coffee?" *Oh brilliant, goof. It's Starbucks.* She quelled the urge to roll her eyes.

"What else?" A lopsided grin spread over his mouth. "And I'd hoped you'd be here."

"Me? Why?" She almost bit her tongue. Was she really that socially challenged?

He chuckled, a pleasant bass note that sent butterflies fluttering in her stomach. "I wanted a name to go with that beguiling smile."

"Oh." *He's so incredibly cute.* When was the last time a man noticed her over a calculation? *Too long*. In spite of the warmth creeping its way up her neck and into her face, she managed a smile.

"Ah, that's what I'm talking about." His eyes sparkled. "Now if only I can get your name, I'll survive my tedious day."

Something about him disarmed her. He was funny and she liked him. "You first. I'll tell you mine if you tell me yours," she teased.

"So that's how we're playing it. John Medina, student and lover of beauty."

She laughed. "Cassie Priam."

"No kidding? Secretary Priam's daughter?" His eyes widened almost imperceptibly, but she noticed. With her dad as the secretary of state, she'd gotten a lot of that here. Cassie hoped the connection wouldn't put John off.

"The one and only." She watched for the usual response, rigid stance, eyes glazed with fear, perspiration followed by a sudden recollection of a previous commitment.

John's gaze didn't falter, but softened. "That's got to be tough."

"I'm used to it," she lied.

* * *

Cassie sipped her coffee in a daze on the way to class. John Medina was a brave man, barely flinching when he'd heard her name. But he wouldn't be interested in her, not really. He hadn't asked her out, and had *player* stamped on his compelling half grin. She must not be his type.

Who was she kidding? Cassie wasn't anyone's type. Her long list of break-ups was proof of that. Medina probably had a string of girls, all of them *beguiling* in some way. *What a line.* At least he hadn't made a run for it right after his order filled. He'd talked to her for another five minutes before escaping with his cup of double-shot latte. She sighed. The man had class. And such a nice smile.

Sipping her mocha, she claimed a seat near the back amid two dozen young men with only a smattering of women sprinkled in. Many would be engineering students, some math majors, and a few had designs in scientific fields. All of them were steady, responsible people and not much fun. *Like me.*

Cassie let the sweet concoction warm her tongue. The little things made life worth living and coffee was one of them. Flirting with a hunky student was another. And flirting was as daring as she'd get. Enough daydreaming.

She set her empty paper cup near her feet and opened her laptop. When she looked up, there stood the elderly professor, tapping her fingers from behind the lectern. "It's time to begin," she drawled. "I'm Professor Simmons and I'll be teaching this section of your class."

Her mind wandered as the slight, graying figure droned. If Cassie couldn't date Medina, at least she could admire him from a distance at Starbucks. Maybe he'd get to know her over coffee and ask her out. Cassie sat up straight and grinned at the thought. He was a student, that should be respectable enough for her parents. Of course, the idea was silly, but there was nothing wrong with using her imagination as long as her feet remained on the ground.

"I forbid it."

"What?" She scanned down her row. All eyes were focused on Simmons. Was she hearing things? It had to be imagination combined with lack of sleep. Cassie focused on the professor and the way her ancient fingers wrapped around the top of the lectern. Nothing like John Medina's hands. She'd noticed how he held his cup with nice capable hands, and she'd liked the look of them.

"I have decreed, and it is so."

The slight accent, his rich tone of voice that held a knife's edge, and underneath an imperious command. The hairs on the back of her neck prickled. That had signaled warning since childhood, or at least, inconvenience. The last time she'd felt that tingle, she'd hiked up Mount Parnassus.

Cassie froze in her seat. Once might be imagination, but hearing voices twice could be signs of mental instability. She glanced over her shoulder. "Did you say something?" she asked the two girls seated behind her. One continued to type on her laptop while the other stared down her nose and shook her head. Still Cassie's neck prickled. *What was it?* The rumble reminded her of those wicked dreams of Apollo. A rush of heat flooded her face.

"Cassandra," the voice whispered into her right ear.

"Oh no," she murmured. The seat beside her was empty, or should be. She stared forward, afraid of what she'd see if she turned her head.

"Look on me."

Heart pinging, she gathered courage and turned to face the voice and her fear. Apollo, shimmering with light from his position beside her, golden mane flowing over his brawny, nude shoulders as if blown by a breeze, his eyes blue as the Adriatic, and that smile. No man should wield such a weapon. It turned her legs to mush.

She shook her head and rubbed her eyes. This couldn't be happening. He had to be a dream or a figment of her imagination. She refused to acknowledge the Greek god. Had she fallen asleep in class? Cassie trained her attention on Simmons. *I am not crazy. It's sleep deprivation, that's all.*

"Beloved." Apollo, clad in a loincloth, his rippling muscles open to inspection, leaned closer.

This delusion was insistent, but Cassie could be just as stubborn She stared forward. *Ignore it and it will go away.* It worked with stray dogs. She must have fallen asleep. That had to be the explanation. *Wake up, Cassie.*

Apollo caressed her jaw with the tips of his fingers. "Must I convince you of my existence each time?"

Her heart thumped and her mouth went dry. *It's not real. It's not real.* He pressed a kiss to that sensitive spot below her ear. She shivered. "Oh God," she murmured. Heat trickled from her neck down to her belly.

"Yes?" His sweet, moist breath warmed her cheek.

Then it hit her. This was different than the dreams. She never smelled anything during those torrid visits as she slept, but now the scent of honey surrounded her. And their interludes always took place lounging on plush cushions under the spreading branches of an olive tree in ancient Greece.

Never in present time.

Her eyes widened. This was no nocturnal fantasy. And if she wasn't losing her mind, then an actual half-naked man nibbled her neck and was doing an excellent job at seduction. She jerked back. "But you're a myth," she argued.

People around her gave her odd looks, and the guy on the other side of her got up and moved. She wanted to sink into the floor. She should just leave and get some fresh air.

"Myth has a basis in fact. Touch and prove me."

An interesting experiment. Cassie held her breath, reached tentative fingers and pushed at his tan chest, satin skin over sculpted muscle and warm flesh. She retracted her trembling hand.

"I am real." His voice had grown smoky. "But

to convince you, I'll share this prophecy: There will be an attack on the American embassy in Greece. Hostages will be taken."

"That's ridiculous," she muttered "We have excellent relations with Greece."

Apollo's gaze darkened to amethyst. "This is a prophecy and warning. Tell your father."

"You've got to be kidding," she said overly loud. All eyes turned and stared at her, puzzled looks on their faces.

"Um, sorry," she said, and got up to leave. Her face burning. "I've got to go." Cassie snatched her laptop and hurried from the room. Heart pounding, tears burning behind her eyes, she fled the room and into the hall with Apollo at her side.

"I'm crazy. Nuts. Insane. Damn it," she said into the air and leaned her back against the wall. "There's no other explanation. I've lost it, and now I won't have to worry about the rest of my life because I'll be committed."

"Cassandra, you're quite sane."

She scowled at him. "Yeah, and I should believe a guy running around in a diaper. I feel so much better."

"I was wrestling with Hermes."

"Figures." She rolled her eyes. "Put some clothes on or, better yet, leave."

"Not until you promise to tell your father of the prophecy."

"Not a chance. Do you really think my dad would believe this tripe?" Her hands tightened around her laptop. "Stay the hell away from me and my father." She moved to leave, but he grabbed her arm, stopping her.

"It's the truth," he growled. "You're my Cassandra and this is your destiny. Share the prophecy. Thwart Hydra."

Cassie was about to stomp on Apollo's sandaled foot when John Medina ran into her, bumping her into the wall.

"Are you all right?" He held onto her with a firm, but gentle grip. "You look upset."

She was far from all right. At least Apollo had disappeared. "I'm fine. Never better."

"Are you sure?" Medina cocked his head to the side. "Do you want to talk about it?"

"Uh, no. Nothing anyone can do."

"Well, if you change your mind. Here's my number." He pulled a card from his jacket pocket and slipped it into her hand. "I've got to get to class." He gave a lopsided smile before striding down the hall.

"What a great guy," she said, and entered his number into her phone.

"I forbid it," the voice grumbled.

Cassie froze. Her mouth tightened in determination. And she finished entering Medina's number.

CHAPTER FOUR

"What the hell?" Cassie muttered as she lowered herself onto a bench outside. The snug pencil skirt tightened around her hips, adding to her discomfort. She sucked in a breath of warm September air scented with fresh-cut lawn. There were only two options—either she was mentally ill, or she was actually being visited by Apollo. Illness was easier to accept.

But a god? How could she resolve the problem? The known factors in this equation were minimal: dreams, hallucinations and hearing voices. Cassie stood, her black pumps firmly anchored on the grass. Logic was the way to solve this. She needed a psychiatrist. Just explain everything and...

The morning headlines appeared in her mind: "Secretary of State's daughter held in mental hospital for observation. Delusional."

"Ugh." She plopped down on the bench, the hard seat adding to her firm resolve. Some would speculate whether insanity ran in the family. She refused to taint her father's political career. It wouldn't do her mother's practice any good either. The situation required more thought.

Seeking medical help might be premature. She should try to solve this herself first. Her jaw cracked from a wide yawn. Since Greece she hadn't enjoyed a full nights rest. Maybe all she needed was a good night's sleep and Apollo would evaporate along with her fatigue. Sleep. That was the logical course. Cassie got to her feet. She'd take a sleep aid and that would be the end of Apollo.

* * *

That night Cassie took two pills and, climbed into bed, and the drag of sleep pulled her under. She stood outside. The night sky blazed with stars like millions of lit candles afloat on a black sea. Cassie breathed in. The scent of lavender mingled with the woodsy smell of cypress and pine igniting her memory. She was dreaming, damn it.

"Beloved."

She recognized the voice and her pulse raced in anticipation. Cassie turned.

Apollo beckoned to her. His thick golden hair cast pale in the moonlight and his crimson robe tied at the waist hung wide and left his chest bare. The lunar glow accentuated every shadow, tempting her gaze to stare and making his masculine features distinct and striking. He looked more like a statue than a mere man until he moved. "Join me upon the couch." Apollo reached out his hand, large, with tapered fingers fit for plucking the strings of his lyre or playing a woman's heart.

She'd visited this secluded spot of forest before in her dreams. They'd sat on cushions and kissed or walked along a path and talked. She couldn't recall much of their conversations, but felt intimacy between them.

He lounged upon a cushion, his smile as tempting as his touch. He may call this a couch, but it was a bed, covered in pillows and silk. This was a dream. Why not enjoy the passion real life had denied her?

Cassie perched on the end of the bed, her hands moist and her mouth dry. She wore a filmy ivory robe that left her arms naked and plunged to her navel. Thin ribbons tied at her shoulders. The fabric barely covered her breasts and gave an illusion of being dressed, but not. She'd never have the guts to wear this outside of a dream.

Apollo sat up and ran his fingertips along her arm raising gooseflesh and longing. How far could she take this fantasy having never experienced everything a man had to offer? She was willing to find out.

"Lie back and close your eyes," he whispered and pressed a wet kiss on the side of her neck.

She shivered. Just that slight touch from his mouth sent warmth through her veins. The bed cradled her. The wisp of silk hid little, her nipples visible, and she moved to cover her breasts with her arms, but he stopped her.

He held her wrists. "Beloved, no harm will come to you, only pleasure. Trust me."

Cassie stared into his blue eyes, sparking with golden light. Waves of desire flooded her. She willed her arms to her sides and closed her eyes. A tickle caressed her skin along her hairline, then the side of her face and over her jaw soft as butterfly wings. "What's that?" she said and stole a peak at him through slit eyes.

He raised a brow. "Close."

She pinched her lids shut.

"A feather," he said. The tip slid down the side of her neck and over he collarbone, leaving a tingle. The sensation stopped. She felt bereft of the feather and wanted to open her eyes and see what he was up to, but forced herself to trust him.

The wisp of feather played over her lips and her tongue swiped to ease the tickle. The feather danced at the edge of fabric covering her breasts. She trembled but remained quiet. She'd never felt so much with so little. Her senses heightened to where his moist breath on her skin was a potent caress. Her pulse picked up and her nipples hardened. He tickled down to her navel. Cool air blew over her thigh and the gossamer robe hiked up and pooled around her hips. A slow tickle slid around her knee and then took a path up the inside of her thigh. She sucked in a breath. Desire heated her core. She bit her bottom lip and moaned.

Apollo took her mouth with his, slow seductive swipes with his tongue teasing her and she arched her neck wanting more. The weight of his warm hand covered her breast.

She woke with her core pulsing with need. "Damn it all to hell," she muttered.

By morning Cassie was exhausted and satisfied. Most of the night spent in the arms of a myth that stoked her fire and teased until she thought she'd scream. This dream of Apollo could become an addiction. If she could just find a man like that, able to make love to her all night, she'd gladly give up her virginity to him. She yawned. And sleep.

Cassie stretched. Her muscles were sore. It was the last dream that she could do without, the damn ugly attack on Athens. A shiver ran over her. Stupid sleeping pills didn't help; instead they'd made everything vivid. Not a bad thing when fantasizing of Apollo's kisses, but hell when she'd dreamed of a gun in her face. Her heart pounded. What if this was a prophecy? She should talk to her dad and warn him. She shook her head to rid the thought. Enough of that, she had to get to class. Time to focus on logic and the real world.

She dressed in a navy suit and ran downstairs to breakfast. She'd decided to make the clothes an experiment. Maybe her new attire had something to do with Medina's taking notice of her. She did stick out on campus. Most students dressed in jeans. Whatever the reason for his attention, she wasn't going to mess with what seemed to work. The answer to her problem didn't lie in dreams, but in a tangible man like John Medina.

Her dad sat at the table doodling, a thoughtful habit she'd watched since childhood. "Hi, Dad."

He put down the pen and smiled at her. "Morning, princess. How is school?"

"Fine." Cassie perched on the edge of the chair next to him.

"That's new." He nodded to her navy blazer.

Cassie ran her fingers over the cashmere lapel. "Mom suggested that I try this look."

"Your mother's idea. I see." He ran a careful gaze over her. "Dress for success."

Those are the words her mom had drilled into her as they'd shopped. "Has Mom left?"

"Yes. Something about giving a lecture this morning." He'd taken up his pen and scribbled on a notepad.

Cassie's gaze dropped to the suitcase on the floor beside his chair. "Where are you off to?"

He continued writing. "Greece."

The short hairs at the back of Cassie's neck stood on end, a definite signal of a bad choice. That bit if intuition had warned her many times, but perhaps this time it was wrong. It was only a nightmare, not real. Maybe.

Looking around her, everything was efficient and based in fact, especially her dad. The sleek furnishings and her father's no-nonsense attitude screamed order, but not Cassie. Her hair had already escaped her clip. "But Dad, Greece?"

"What is it, sweetheart?" He covered her hand with his and patted with gentle reassurance.

"I, um. Is it the right time to go to Greece?" She pulled up the corners of her mouth, trying for confident. What was she doing? She'd had a weird dream, that's all.

He cocked his well-coiffed salt and pepper head. "This is work, not a vacation."

She cleared her throat. "I don't believe it's a good idea."

"Why? Is it because of the news about the Middle East? You know the media, they sensationalize everything."

She shrugged against the stiff fabric of the suit. "Just a feeling."

"A feeling?" His brows hiked up. "Since when do you rely on feelings? Facts are what matter, and the fact is I'm needed in Greece." He stared into her face, his hazel eyes were soft with concern. "What's this really about?"

How could she tell him? She valued her dad's good opinion and longed for his respect. Putting herself out there with a ridiculous prophetic utterance could ruin it all. Cassie shook her head. Telling her dad that she had a hunch about Greece sounded like a cry for attention. She was pretty sure she didn't believe any of the assault on the embassy. It was fantasy. Her father didn't go in for anything but facts. He refused to trust a feeling. No way would she tell him that a god visited her.

Yeah, that would go over big. She'd be scheduled for a long vacation and psychological testing. Not going there. "Is it safe?"

He laughed. "It's Greece. Of course it's safe. I have security and won't be gone long." He leaned closer and squeezed her hand. "Stop worrying. You're beginning to sound like your mother."

Cassie hoped not. She loved her mom, but she did not want to act like her. "No, it's not that." Maybe the sleeping pills had left her muddled and there was nothing more to it.

"Glad to hear it. You've been on edge since you returned from your trip. Is it the break-up? That last young man wasn't worth your time. You just need to get out and meet new people. You'll be fine." He stood and pressed a kiss to the top of her head. "Have to catch a flight. See you in a few days."

She remained mute, watching him grab his suitcase and leave. Bad enough she'd almost made a fool of her self with that stupid "prophecy" about Greece, but her father saw her as a kid moping over that idiot Eric. Sure, getting dumped hurt—again. But it didn't devastate her or keep her up at night. Or did it? Is that what Apollo was all about? How better to mend her wounded pride than to enjoy the attentions of a sexy god? Damn. She really did need to start dating. That would end it.

She straightened her shoulders and made a decision. She wouldn't say anything about Apollo or Greece. Her dad knew the situation in the Middle East. Cassie stood, having lost her appetite. And no wonder — telling the secretary of state how to do his job, that would be crazy.

* * *

Apollo viewed Cassie's inaction with supreme annoyance from his invisible vantage point at her side. As god of prophecy, he knew she'd doubt, but knowing didn't make her lack of faith more palatable — it tasted bitter as gall.

If she didn't believe in her gift, no one else would. That had been the problem at Troy. He hadn't cursed her gift beyond stripping away her confidence. It had worked — too well, making all the difference. They both had suffered greatly for it.

He lowered his head, burdened with guilt as heavy as Earth straining Atlas' broad shoulders. Three thousand years ago, Apollo had watched her torment until it swamped her mind and destroyed her. *Not this time. I swear by Olympus, not this time.* He fisted his hands. Hating the helplessness of his position, a position he'd agreed to in order to bring Cassandra from the depths of Hades to life and give him another chance at love. This time, he'd win her heart.

She walked passed him, hips swaying under the straight wool, breasts pushing against fabric. He wasn't accustomed to seeing her dressed thusly: restrained elegance that strived to hide her sexuality and had failed miserably. The skirt hugged her shapely backside, and each stride of her long legs drew his eye to those delicious curves. The blouse and jacket, both clung to her trim waist and flowed over her breasts like water. These garments didn't conceal but did the opposite, making the soft swell of rosy skin above the neckline and each intake of breath a temptation to touch. The woman shouldn't dress as an open invitation, not when other men would view her as he did; a goddess wrapped tight begging to be unfurled. And one man in particular, that cropped student. Had she no sense? What could that mortal offer? He'd end that soon enough.

Her scent, almond oil mixed with her own nectar still lingered, calling to him in ways that heated his blood and desire. Did she conspire to drive men mad? After seeing her administer the lotion to her delicate flesh, he couldn't smell the concoction without recalling her silken skin, the perfection of her body and his need. He'd speak to her about her clothing and intoxicating aroma, and then her future.

How to change her fate and that of a nation? Zeus forbade his outright interference. Apollo could deliver visions, dreams and prophecy of impending doom, but not alter men's hearts or their actions. His gift of divination told him Cassie waited. For what, a sign?

What did she require beyond the proof of her

eyes and the touch of her hand on his warm chest? Visitation from a god once brought mortals to their knees, but not in this age. His jaw tightened. She doubted, not herself alone, but in the very existence of the gods of Mount Olympus, and the idea of a power mightier than mortal's puny science.

"Science." He spit the word into the air like a gnat caught between his teeth. The gods created science. Willful, arrogant mortals, did they think themselves superior to the forces of the heavens and Zeus? Ah, the ignorance and vanity of men. They needed instruction. Apollo followed her outside unseen, but she should have sensed him.

Her lack proved Cassandra was no different: she believed only in facts. Powerful gods didn't exist in her world. It would be his task to convince her. A few demonstrations were in order. Not in wrath, as he'd often done, but with patience. He had to woo the girl. The wager he'd made with Hades required gaining her love, if he failed.... Apollo shuddered. He wouldn't think of it. Some losses were too great for even a god to bear.

* * *

Cassie felt eyes on her, though she was alone in the car. It had to be her imagination on steroids thanks to her fuzzy brain. "Ugh." She'd missed another parking place. What was her problem today? Her head felt packed with marshmallows and thoughts of the sexy half-naked god. She couldn't avoid dreaming about him and couldn't make him budge from her mind.

It had to be the sleeping pills. Sleep was nice but the price seemed high, maybe too high. Thoughts of Apollo distracted and warmed her, obliterating her focus. If she had to have an imaginary friend, why a Greek god dipped in testosterone? Maybe she'd missed her calling and should write romance novels for lonely women lacking a social life—*like me*. Her dad was right; she needed to get out more.

"Freakin' fantastic." Cassie slipped into an empty parking slot and hurried to class. She needed her ordered life back, a clear head, and wanted Apollo reduced to minus. A vision of the god nibbling her neck made her skin tingle. Enough lurid daydreaming, she was late for class.

She quickened her pace.

Cassie tiptoed in, taking a seat in the last row. The professor explained the lesson and she flipped open her laptop to take notes. One word flashed in bold red across the screen, Greece. Greece. Greece. She slammed it shut. "Holy crap."

Heads turned, eyes glaring in reprimand for the interruption. Cassie sunk lower in her seat. Her stomach knotted. "Please, let it be gone," she murmured. With trembling fingers, she inched her laptop open.

Did you say something?" asked the skinny guy next to her.

Heat filled her face. "Oh, just thinking out

loud."

She glared at the screen, daring it to misbehave. The expected lesson glared back.

A sigh of relief escaped her tense lips. Leaning back, she let her hair fall behind her, brushing along the back of the seat. What if he was more than a diversion from loneliness and a damaged ego? What if there really was a man like Apollo, not a god or figment, but someone she'd glimpsed? Warmth filled her core and she licked her lips.

But she trusted logic. That's what made life work, not stolen kisses under an olive tree from another time. Ah, but what kisses, the kind that belonged to sultry nights and willing flesh, and creating longing she'd never know before. Cassie stared at her computer in an effort to push the desire from her mind and failed. Such a man was everything she'd wanted. What if he was the love she'd waited for all this time, and why no other relationship worked out?

No. Absolutely not. Cassie shook her head in firm denial. She could not, would not allow this invasion into her mind. She sounded ridiculous, crazy, in heat. If this was a weird reaction from those damn sleeping pills, she refused to take them again. Nope, not happening. Besides, why wait for a dream to manifest when a flesh and blood hunky student might be available? Her parents might approve of Medina. He looked responsible: none of the long hair and unkempt attire of most students. He might even have a job. And he'd given her his number. That made sense.

Her nape prickled as if icy fingers stroked her skin. She reached up and rubbed away the chill. Good thing Apollo was the stuff of dreams. Only something monumental could force her to accept the existence of delicious Greek gods and prophecy. Monumental didn't seem likely. Life was best lived in full view, with feet on the ground and a clear head. Cassie determined to embrace reality. And Medina was real and had soulful dark eyes. Besides, what were the chances of a real man like Apollo showing up or an attack at the embassy? Like her dad said: It's Greece, of course it was safe.

CHAPTER FIVE

Cassie bolted upright in bed, skin covered with sweat and her heart slamming against her ribs. The damp yellow t-shirt clung to her. Nightmares of Troy's destruction had haunted her on occasion since her teens, but never like this. The dream had morphed into present-day Athens. Sleeping pills didn't stop them.

Pictures of the American embassy, gunmen spraying corridors with bullets, and the wounded left where they fell, all branded her mind. It didn't matter that the dream had ended; she still saw their anguished faces staring back with glassy eyes when she closed her lids. She trembled and fisted her sheets. In rare night visions of Troy, she'd watched carnage from a safe distance like viewing a movie...but this.

She pulled her legs to her chest hugging them close. Not in this version. It drew her into the nightmare. Shots echoed through the building, panicked screams ringing in her ears. She'd cowered behind an office door—listening. Down the hall, people sobbed and guns fired, followed by deafening silence. The coppery smell of blood filled her nose. A barrage of hard-healed shoes pounded outside her hiding place. Gooseflesh covered her arms. Her breath stilled. In the dream, she focused on the door, too terrified to make a sound, legs trembling as adrenaline pumped into her with nowhere to run. The knob turned and…

Cassie buried her face against her quivering knees. *It's a dream. Just a terrible dream.*

"It's a prophecy."

She screamed.

Her head sprung up in the direction of the intruder, heart racing, pulse pounding in her ears. "Damn you," she grumbled, and scowled at Apollo. "I thought I was awake. What are you doing here?"

"I've come to help. I see you doubt me and the warning." The man dressed in a white tunic, a bronze breastplate covering his broad chest. He carried a bow with a quiver of arrows slung over his shoulder. As in all her dreams of the god, he looked the part.

"If you want to help, leave me alone."

"You don't mean that."

"Oh yes I do." She nabbed a pillow and clutched it to her chest. "Your kind of help I can do without. Besides, I've decided that you're not real. You can't be."

"It matters not what you've decided to believe. I am real. Here I stand."

"Like that's proof? No one else has seen you."

"You want me to appear to others?"

She shrugged. "They do say 'seeing is believing'."

"I can't do that."

"Can't? I thought you were a god."

"Zeus forbids displaying ourselves to mortals without permission."

"Of course he does." Cassie rolled her eyes. "How convenient." Apollo left his quiver of arrows and bow hanging in mid-air and sat beside her on the bed. She scooted over and nodded to the suspended implements. "Nice effect."

He ignored the comment. "Cassandra." His voice slid over her like warm chocolate. "I've warned you and now you've seen the violence destined for Athens. Only you have the power to stop it."

Apollo was beautiful, and in her dreams his kisses curled her toes, but she'd had this conversation. "People don't believe this stuff, not unless you're a phone psychic with a name like Sybil."

He cocked his golden head. "I never cared much for Sybil. She uttered from a rock rather than my sacred temple."

"Ugh. Focus. I'm pretty sure that you're not real, and I need to get up early for class. You can leave now. Trust me, no one will listen to this warning."

Apollo rested his chin on the back of his hand, light-brown brows drawn low in concentration.

His pose reminded her of the statue The Thinker, only Apollo was better looking. "Because you lack faith, and there's time before the embassy falls, I'll give you a small revelation as proof."

"And then you'll let me sleep?" She breathed out exasperated. "Fine."

He rewarded her with a smile. "At nine in the morning, a man carrying a pink rose will seek you out."

Cassie yawned. "It doesn't count if you're the guy."

"His name is John."

"Really?" She must have perked up too much based on Apollo's warm blue gaze changing to glacial ice. Cassie lost the excited tone and tried to look disinterested. "What does he say?"

Apollo pressed his lips together. "It doesn't matter. You tell him no."

"That's the proof? Your big revelation to convince me to stick my neck out and leave my dad thinking I have a screw loose is a guy with a flower?"

"It's enough. The point is that it occurs as I've told you."

"I guess." She leaned against the padded cream fabric headboard. "Nine. Rose. John. Got it."

Apollo took her small hand in his large one and pressed his soft lips to her knuckles. The contact made her lightheaded. "One more thing, Cassandra," he whispered, leveling his gaze on her. "You're mine. Best for all if you heed that fact."

* * *

Time had always meant schedules, but rarely controlled her thoughts. Cassie checked the time on her phone—again. Five minutes to nine. And then what? Was she supposed to accept an alternate reality as fact?

She wasn't the type to pray, but she hoped John wouldn't walk into the coffee shop, pink rose or not. Ridding herself of this version of a god complex would be a relief. Another minute passed. "I can't take it," she grumbled, got up from her chair, strode to the bakery case, and stared at oversized muffins. At ten after nine, she was out of there. Enough of this silliness.

Cassie chewed her thumb. A nervous habit her mom despised. Like lives depended on well cared-for cuticles and smooth edges. Her reflection taunted her in the glass. Nothing about her was smooth.

Today's costume of tan jacket and slacks stifled her as much as yesterday's navy. She looked the part of masters student unless you paid close attention. She'd lost the battle with her hair and let it cascade over her shoulders to her waist. *Not professional.* Her mom, unfortunately paid close attention to her daughter's appearance.

Cassie tried to do the right thing but inevitably failed. Her mom wanted her to attend medical school. Her dad shoved politics at her. And Cassie longed to immerse herself in the safety of predictable calculations. No surprises for her. She wanted logic and order. So why had she invented this strange fixation with Apollo? It was so unlike her. Lingering in fragrant gardens with a god and sharing kisses in the moonlight was wonderful, but experiencing the disturbing attack on the embassy chilled her blood. She shivered. *It couldn't be real. Could it?*

"Hello."

Damn.

She sighed and turned around, ready to deal with fate. John Medina ordered his double- shot latte and then flashed his grin on Cassie. Those butterflies in her stomach took flight, propelled by the power of his deep brown eyes. They crashed in flames when she realized John Medina proved Apollo's existence and the prophecy. Her stomach knotted.

Wait one minute, John showed up there for coffee most every day. It didn't mean anything. There was still the detail of a pink rose and she didn't see one. If everything happened as Apollo had said, then she'd have to believe in the gods and prophecy, but it would mess with all she knew.

John strode toward her, pulling out something from inside his jacket. A small pink rose. "For you."

Just as Apollo said. Damn. Had she seen Apollo

and touched him? Cassie trusted her own senses, but her head swam from the bizarre thought. The Olympian gods were real? She had to get hold of herself. If Apollo was real, then the embassy might fall and she'd have to do something.

He smiled and handed her the flower. "I'd hoped you'd be here."

Her skin chilled and she breathed deep to fight sudden nausea. *I'm fine. Get it together and say something.* "You were looking for me?" She put her thumb to her lips and nibbled.

"I wanted to ask you to lunch." His adorable lopsided grin distracted her enough from her realization to settle her stomach.

She curbed her nail biting and dropped her hand to her side. Cassie liked John. Her dad thought she needed to meet more people, and no regular guy was beating down her door asking for a date. Apollo didn't count. Regular didn't begin to describe him. And John was just so cute. "Lunch would be great."

A flash of light.

Oh no. Cassie blinked. Apollo floated behind John, his muscular arms crossed over his bare chest. He glared blue daggers at John's back. "What are you doing?" he growled. "Tell him no."

Cassie casted her gaze past the fuming god to the girl making John's order. She hadn't heard anything.

Neither had John. "About one?" he asked.

"Sure." Cassie struggled to ignore the deity and grinned at hunky buzzcut. Apollo's gaze darkened. That made her nervous. Cassie shoved her hands into the pockets of her slacks. Ticking off a god might be a bad idea, but she'd been told what to do her entire life and she'd had enough. "I have to take a short lunch. Can we meet at the grill in the Leavy Center?"

"Okay, but that's not much of a date."

"I'm sorry." Here it came, the dump. Every one of her romantic relationships had ended before they moved on to something serious. Why should Mr. Adorable be any different? Maybe she was cursed. "Do you want to forget it?"

"No. If we have to settle for a quick lunch, then I want to take you to dinner, too."

"Um." Cassie thought she saw flames flickering in Apollo's eyes. That *had* to be her imagination. "We can discuss it at lunch."

John crinkled his brow. "Is everything okay? You don't seem very excited. Are you seeing someone?"

"Not really." She ran her hand through her hair. "It ended ages ago."

"Ah, I see. He won't let it go." John shook his head. "The past is past."

"Not for some people."

"I can't blame the guy. Any man would be a fool to let you go." John winked. "See you at one."

* * *

Apollo shot from Earth to the heavenly realms in such a white-hot beam of light, his sandals smoked. Zeus glanced at him sideways and continued his game of chess using mortal pawns.

"The impudence," Apollo grumbled. Cassandra had accepted an invitation from a man with *him* standing there. *I'm a god.* What could she want with a weak mortal when she had Apollo pledging love?

He strode to the table where Zeus played chess against his brother, Hades. "Not going well?" Hades smirked. His chalky skin paled against his black tunic.

Apollo leveled a seething glare. "There's time."

"Yes, I can wait to collect the wager." Hades' gray lips stretched into a disturbing grin. "A year of you servitude in the underworld is better than when Hermes gained your sacred cattle."

Apollo's anger flared and Hades covered his face with the hood of his garment against the heat. Light burst from Apollo's body. A usual occurrence when strong emotion took over.

"Apollo, Hades. Stop this." Zeus slammed his meaty fist on the marble table, making the chess pieces quake. "You two made a wager. I've bound you both to stand by it. No more tormenting your nephew, Hades. Apollo will succeed."

Apollo cooled to a soft glow. Hades lowered the dusky cloth from his face, brushed the smoldering ash from his garment and considered the chessboard, refusing to meet Apollo's eyes.

Zeus moved his knight, a mortal, the secretary of state for the United States. Hades scowled. Zeus, ever confident, leaned back in his Roman chair and stretched. "You can't beat me, brother. You're a god, but I rule here." Zeus turned his attention to Apollo. "What brings you?"

"Give me permission to remove one mortal."

"You know the law. Is this human destined to die?"

Apollo clenched his jaw. His father would have to ask. "The Fates say not yet, but he's a problem."

"He?" Zeus tilted his silver-haired head.

"John Medina. A loathsome rodent."

Zeus scratched his head. His moss-green eyes sparkled with amusement. Apollo had seen this restrained humor often, usually at his expense. "Don't tell me that a mere mortal man has you worried?"

"Certainly not. He's an annoyance, a fly teetering on the edge of a glass of fine wine. Allow me to squash the insect before he ruins the brew."

Hades chuckled. The sound was reminiscent of screeching bats. "Ah, Cassandra favors your fly. How dismal for you."

Apollo ignored his uncle and focused on Zeus. "All mortals die and he has no great bearing on the future. It's only one rodent."

"The law is the law, my son. Do you wish to tempt the Fates?"

Apollo grumbled under his breath. "Might I at least move this man to another location?"

"You can't force him." Hades shook his head of stringy dull hair. "It's his choice."

"He'll be persuaded." Apollo lowered his brows at his uncle.

"You think much of your skills," said Hades.

"I convinced you to release Cassandra from the underworld."

"Or were you the one convinced, nephew?" Hades moved his rook, represented by a creature called Hydra.

Zeus raised one thick brow. "Interesting decision."

Apollo chafed against his uncle's rebuff. "I'll win Cassandra's heart and the wager. When I do, Hades, you'll bow and scrape under my command."

Hades set his black gaze on Apollo. "We shall see, boy. We shall see."

CHAPTER SIX

Cassie perused the restaurant's offerings stretched out before her in sleek steel trays as she waited for Mr. Tasty Buzzcut. Being raised by type A parents, she'd learned to be early for everything. Great for school and work, but when it came to parties and dates, not so much. Today it gave her a chance to wrap her head around having her first date in far too long.

Medina was a student. That wouldn't impress her dad. She hoped he had a job. Her parents might relax if he passed inspection and proved reliable. Few men had the inclination or the balls to stand up to scrutiny. And she didn't know anything about him other than he had a grin that needed kissing. Could this budding relationship bloom?

Fat chance.

She'd be lucky if John showed up for lunch, much less dinner. *Dinner.* She hadn't agreed to that, thank goodness. If they hit it off, and if he wasn't using her to further his career, and if she didn't get that warning prickle at the back of her neck, and if he stuck around long enough to know her, then maybe they could move to the next level. "A lot of ifs," she mumbled.

The next level would be sex, and a first. Her face glowed with warmth at the thought of moving from reluctant virgin to initiate of a romantic coupling. Oh, who was she kidding? Even in her dreams of Apollo they'd never gotten down to enjoying each other fully. There had to be something wrong with her. She didn't know anyone her age that hadn't experienced sex. It wasn't for lack of wanting to fall in love, but the men had decided that she wasn't worth their time.

Apollo was more than a man and deserved his own category. The god toyed, kissed, caressed, nuzzled and spoke sweet words to her, but held back before intimacy. Did she have perpetual bad breath and they couldn't stand exposure? Cassie held her hand to her face and blew air, smelling for offensive odor. Minty fresh. Bad breath wasn't the problem. It had to be her.

And what about Apollo? He'd looked beyond annoyed when John had asked her out. She'd never seen anyone's eyes smolder like hot coals before. Creepy. Maybe dangerous. And real. *And real. Shit.* Cassie shook her head. The prophecy had to be just as solid, but she had no idea of what to do about the embassy. Tell her dad? Yeah, right. She couldn't just blurt it out. Cassie needed to think it through and have a logical plan. And she'd focus on that right after her lunch.

She scanned the cafeteria for John. Wood-grain Formica tables' hosted men and women in an array of dress, others congregated at the drink dispenser, and a few stood in line placing their orders. The hum of conversation and smell of sizzling food brought memories of sitting at a similar table with her dad. Her mom would've disapproved, had she been there. Suggesting salad over the salty food and the milkshake Cassie loved. Her dad once told her that magic and memories weren't built on things as flimsy as lettuce. They required substance, something solid like meat, potatoes and plenty of salt and sugar. Cassie licked her lips.

"Hey beautiful." John strode toward her, wearing that lopsided grin that made her heart flutter. "What will you have?"

A mischievous smile spread over her mouth. "A burger, fries and a diet cola."

He chuckled and the bass note played over her like fingers stroking. "That's what I like to see, a woman that eats real food. Not that I'm against veggies, just not as a meal."

John got in line to place their order and Cassie snagged a small table that gave her a fine view of John's back. Broad shoulders, athletic build, no telling about his butt, but she'd bet it was tight and well formed under his jacket. She let herself imagine him in a Roman toga. *Nice legs.*

Enough of that. Indulging in daydreams wouldn't help. There was more to a person than looks. He might be a workaholic, a womanizer, an opportunist, or as boring as green salad with fat-free dressing on the side. She raked her gaze over him. He didn't look like salad. John appeared to be a man that enjoyed a challenge. Would he be any different from the other men she'd gone out with?

Her stomach rumbled. Cassie sucked in a breath of delicious French fry scented air to steady herself. Better to find out now before she invested herself.

John set the food-laden tray on the table and slid into his seat, his burnt-umber eyes sparkling. "Ketchup?"

"Please." Cassie took a packet from his hand brushing his fingers. A tingle went up her arm from the slight contact. They had chemistry and just sitting close to him made her head float like a cloud.

He took a swig from his drink and leveled his gaze on her. "Tell me about yourself. And you can bypass all the stuff about your father. I want to hear about you."

That was a first, for as long as she could remember conversations always centered on her very important dad. This man piqued her interest. "There isn't much to tell."

"A woman so captivating has to have history."

Heat filled her face and she hoped he didn't notice her blush. "I'm getting my Masters. I'm a bit of a math nerd." Not at all impressive or fun.

She had to come up with something better than that. "I spent the summer in Europe. Greece was my favorite."

He took a bite of his double cheeseburger, nodding as he chewed and swallowed. "That's interesting. It doesn't sound like you're planning to follow in your father's footsteps."

"Politics? No way. I want a PhD and to teach at a university."

"Beauty and brains. Don't often find those pared." His grin widened. "My goals are to finish my masters and work for the FBI. I interned for them last summer. I'm a computer geek. I chose Georgetown to gain the right connections." He shrugged his shoulders. "I get the math nerd thing, so don't feel weird about it. Computer geek isn't very exciting, but the FBI is. Meeting the right people is all part of getting ahead."

Right connections? *Red flag.* He could be an opportunist. Cassie looked up from her burger and he continued. "I have big plans."

Cassie dabbed her mouth with the white paper napkin. "And what do you hope to do, run the FBI?"

He leaned forward in his plastic seat, his eyes glossed. "Maybe, when I get older. But for now, I hope to work in cyber terrorism. Stop the bastards and maybe infiltrate them and take down their systems. Make a name for myself. It gets my heart and mind racing just thinking about it."

"That sounds exciting."

"Sure, there's some of that, but what my goals really require is careful planning. I love the control it takes to figure out systems and access codes. I can't wait to get out of school and really accomplish something."

"You sound motivated."

"Got to be, if you want to get anywhere in this world. I have plans."

She bet he did. The kind of plans that included using her as a rung on his ladder. Just as she'd feared, another relationship that was over before it started. *User*. Cassie stabbed at her ketchup with a French fry.

Love appeared unlikely, but not impossible. John had noticed her before he knew her name. There wasn't anything wrong with ambition. Her dad was ambitious. And her mother breathed her successful practice. She should at least give Medina a chance. That was more than most men had given her. Two dates and gone. That was the average. But she refused to be stupid about this. Why wait to be dumped and suffer the ensuing pain? Why not just get it all out there and if he ran, better now than later.

She sat up straight and strived to sound confident. "So, is using me to get to my dad part of your plan?"

John sputtered soda and coughed. "Whoa. Are you always this direct?" He cleared his throat. "Honestly, it wouldn't hurt to know your dad, but I don't need him. I have a job waiting for me when

I finish school. When I saw you at Starbucks the only plan I had was to ask you out."

Cassie wasn't sure that she believed him, but his brown eyes were soft and he had that adorable repentant puppy look down. "I just wanted to be clear. It's nothing personal."

"You've been burned before."

"Fried."

John reached across the table and covered her hand with his. "I'm not going to hurt you."

The back of her neck prickled and then the tingle spread over her entire body. Was this a huge warning or the beginning of a long-term relationship? Maybe both?

* * *

Apollo watched unseen from the abode of the gods as Cassie sighed over that puffed up, excuse for a man. The fool nodded his head and salivated at the chance to make a name for himself. Cassie was part of this mortal's plan. And if thwarting the relationship needed a shove from a god, then so be it. Apollo had a heart to win.

Streaking through space, Apollo arrived at the Leavy Center and hovered above the pair, feeling the scowl transform his features. He might not be able to remove this human, but he could enjoy himself at his expense. The rodent reached for his paper cup and, with help, knocked it over, spilling sticky, brown liquid over himself. That should end the conversation.

The man dabbed at his clothing with wads of paper napkins and stood to swath his darkening slacks. Apollo grinned at the display until Cassie rose to help. She wiped the man's jacket and lower across his belt. Was the woman so naive? This John creature grinned at her attentions and she continued administrating the napkin down the front of his slacks.

Enough. This activity had to stop. Apollo planted himself behind the human in line with Cassie's vision, but invisible to all others. Her eyes grew round. She ended her stroking of the man's slacks and stood. "I think we got most of it." She smiled at the rodent.

"Not a problem. I've some clothes in my car, but I better get changed and head to class." John snapped up the tray soiled with brown, soaked napkins. "I'll pick you up at your house at seven."

"Can't wait." She beamed at the man.

Apollo felt heat flare in his eyes. Annoyance filled his chest and flowed through his limbs. That adoring look belonged to him, not that measly human. The man left and Cassie glared at Apollo. Not the look he'd wanted.

"Proud of yourself?" She whispered the words through her teeth.

"Is it my fault that mortal is clumsy?"

Her violet eyes narrowed. "I'm guessing 'yes'." She tipped her chin up and stomped away.

He'd had women turn from him. One ran, preferring the form of a laurel tree to avoid his ardor, but that had been millennia ago. And Cassie was human. She should have laughed at his antics, not derided him. Had women changed so much since he'd visited Earth?

He waited to see if she'd stop and glance at him. Cassie sped her stride. His heart sank. Apparently mortal females no longer found his playfulness charming. Or was it only Cassie? Apollo's gaze continued to follow her form. She stopped. His heart swelled. If she would turn and smile at him, then he'd know she only played at being angry. But she didn't turn. Cassie paused, rubbed the back of her neck and walked on.

Perhaps she wanted to be pursued. She had stopped her escape and that moment of hesitation on her part was all the proof he needed. Her pride stood between them. That's what it was. She played with him. He did enjoy all manner of sport. *And my Cassandra knows this.* He'd join in her game. Females shied from being too easily won, and he would win. If she wanted the chase to go on a little longer, before her pride allowed her to succumb, so be it. He had time to indulge her—for now.

* * *

Cassie fumed all the way to her next class. How dare he? That arrogant, self-serving excuse for a god. This idiotic behavior at John's expense had to stop. Wasn't it enough that she was stuck with this gift of prophecy and she'd have to decide on a course of action? The damn vision of blood and destruction scared the hell out of her. She had to act. She turned her gaze heavenward. "Thank you for the gift," she muttered through her teeth. "Leave me alone."

She'd find a way to warn her dad and then cut Apollo loose before he could ruin her chance at a normal relationship. But how? Her dad had already left for Greece. The attack might occur any moment. It might be too late. Tension tightened her jaw and a shudder ran through her body. No. Not happening. There had to be time to stop the attack. Otherwise, why tell her about it? She needed to persuade her dad and then convince him to do something. Not easy. The man was stubborn as rocks. Sending an email was ridiculous. She had to call him. Beg and plead if she had to. And if that didn't work? Bitterness filled her mouth and she swallowed hard. Why didn't Apollo appear to her dad? That would've made sense. Why torment her with this prophecy and the task of stopping it? Nothing about Apollo made sense. She'd like to string him up by that diaper he paraded around in. "Big, selfish baby."

Staring at her laptop, Cassie couldn't focus on the professor, but typed out her argument for her dad. She had to build a case. She dug through the news, all the information on the volatile Middle East, anything that might lend weight to her plea. He had to believe her.

＊

Cassie took a break from class at three in the afternoon, skedaddled to the privacy of her car and called her dad on her cell phone. She had to reach him before her date or it would be the middle of the night in Athens. That last dream had shaken her. The memory of automatic weapon fire still pounded in her head.

The phone rang.

And rang.

"I'm sorry, but I'm unavailable to take your call. Please leave a message…"

Cassie cut off and tried her dad's phone again, but received the same irritating message.

"Damn it," she muttered as she went for another go at reaching him. "Pick up. Pick up. Pick up."

It rang, went into message and she ended the call.

Cassie scanned her notes. She couldn't give up. All those people would die if she didn't get through to her dad. He must be in a meeting. What was it, ten at night in Greece? Meetings weren't held that late. Maybe a social gathering. "Ugh. Where are you?"

She called again.

And again.

Cassie continued for fifteen minutes and…

"Cassie? Why didn't you leave a message?"

"Hi Dad. Why didn't you answer your

phone?" Her relief at reaching him ended as she geared up to tell him her reason for the call.

"I answered. I'm speaking to you, aren't I?"

"Um, yes." Her throat tightened and she cleared it. "I know this might seem unlikely, but hear me out. I've come across information that our embassy in Athens is in danger of attack."

Silence met her warning.

"Dad?"

"Yes." He sighed. "Did your mother put you up to this to get me home?"

"Mom? No." It did sound like something her mother would do.

"And when is this supposed to take place?"

She could almost hear him shaking his head at her. "I'm not sure, but soon."

"Where did you come up with this?"

Her stomach twisted. She knew he'd have to ask that. "I can't say."

"Is this another *feeling*?"

Damn.

Cassie wanted to punch something, preferably a god in a diaper. "Dad, this is real. You have to believe me and close the embassy. Get out of Greece before people are killed."

Silence.

"This sounds serious," he said. "I'll make you a deal. I'll check into intel regarding our embassy if you promise to do something for me."

Her dad cutting deals was never a good sign. But what choice did she have? "Okay. What do you want?"

"Make an appointment for yourself with Dr. Malvo."

"Mom's therapist?" Oh, hell.

"Yes. Those are my conditions. I'm concerned."

"Fine," she grumbled into her phone. "I'll call her in the morning and you'll check this out. Right?" Forget punching Apollo, she'd rather shoot him for getting her into this situation.

"Of course. Good night, princess. I'll call you at five your time tomorrow night."

"Good night, Dad." The call ended.

That went worse than expected. She knew he'd be difficult to convince, but now Cassie had to see Dr. Sylvia Malvo and be evaluated.

"Damn Apollo."

At least she had something to look forward to. A date with tasty John Medina.

* * *

Hours dragged on to five o'clock and leaving her last class for home. And her date, dinner with a man that might be honest, could be as full of it as her last failure. Not every guy was a flake. She had friends who'd met great guys. Some were serious and looking forward to marriage. Not her.

John had appeared interested before Apollo dumped the drink in his lap. *Jerk.* She hadn't seen that neanderthal behavior since high school. She didn't appreciate it then, and less so now. Were all men little boys? Eric had lasted longer than most and then no explanation or official break-up. He just didn't call. *Like the others*. A steady ache spread through her chest.

Cassie hadn't been willing to let it go. She'd invested her heart and her future in Eric. She'd called him, texted, sent him emails. No answers. In desperations she'd stalked him, hoping to confront the coward and find out what happened.

That was a low moment.

He'd threatened her with a restraining order. Imagine. All she'd wanted was closure. An explanation of why he'd walked away without the courtesy of a goodbye. Well, she'd gotten closure—and a hard slam to her ego. Eric looked uneasy when he'd seen her, but not sorry. There were words for men like him, but she didn't use that kind of language in public. And he wasn't worth demeaning herself further. Time to move on, but she had to be on her guard. John might dump her once he found the dull truth of her. Men didn't want her, not for long.

Except Apollo.

Yes, he was gorgeous and he knew it. He said beautiful things, praised her looks and her eyes, but never once her intelligence. Still, taken as a whole, he'd be worth risking a chance. She shook her head. And why was she entertaining this messed-up relationship anyway? It couldn't work. Apollo was a god. The idea went beyond dysfunctional to destructive. *I'm not going there.* He could only be interested in her as a curiosity, and once he grew bored, he'd be gone. Well, messing with her heart wasn't an Olympic sport. Anger's red haze filled her head. She was tired of being played with, and when she next saw that toga-clad child, she'd tell him so.

CHAPTER SEVEN

How did human males function? From his abode in the godly realms, Apollo scowled into the full-sized mirror to access the European fit of his navy suit. The fabric cut close across his flanks and left little to the imagination regarding his masculine assets. With each breath the fabric strained against his chest as if the buttons might fly off like discuses hurled by Heracles. Apollo preferred the cool freedom of ancient dress to this suffocating clothing. In the ancient games they'd worn nothing to restrict them. But this sport required modern trappings. John dressed in this style. Apollo worked his jaw muscles. And Cassandra had smiled at the rodent.

Apollo considered the coat, how it accentuated his broad shoulders, his trim waist, and how the navy hue played up his bright blue eyes. In all, the clothing had merits. Freedom and accessibility weren't among them. But if that measly human could withstand the infringement to his neither regions, so could he.

"What next?" Apollo scanned the list Artemis

had given him: Ways to gain the love of women in this new age. "Suit—done." Cassandra wouldn't need flowers, not when she had him for her eyes to feast upon. "No flowers."

Perfume? He shook his head, dismissing the idea. The woman's scent made his mouth water. Why hide it? "No perfume."

Chocolate? He'd meant to ask Artemis about the form of that gift, but became distracted when she said he needed shearing. His golden waves brushing his shoulders were his crowning glory. How many women had twisted their slender fingers in his long mane while they wrapped their legs around his hips in ecstasy? He smiled at the memories. No. That he refused. He would never come to Cassandra shorn of his beauty.

Apollo scanned the list. "Listen."

That must be important. The goddess had written it in large, gold characters. That he could do. He'd make sure Cassandra listened to him. When he finished speaking, there'd be no doubt in her mind that she belonged to him. The list continued for another page, but Apollo folded the paper and slipped it into his jacket pocket. Enough for now. No need to overwhelm the girl. She'd fall into his arms, declaring her adoration for him.

His uncle was a fool to wager against him. Apollo opened the top two buttons of his crisp white shirt and breathed in. He despised restraints. Physical freedom was part of the joy of being a god. How difficult to live as a mortal prone to illness and death. Fear ruled humanity, shackling them to the illusion of safety at the cost of greatness and freedom. Most wasted their short lives too afraid to follow the seed planted in their bosom urging them toward more, listening instead to other defeated souls as their guides. He shook his head. *Such a dark and slight existence.*

Cassandra desired more of life. Passion burst from her. He felt it each time she argued with him. She fought to nurture her true self against her parents and the world. Her courage in Troy had won Apollo's case with the gods and gained her spirit's release from Hades. Few mortals displayed god-like virtue. Courage and determination were part of what he loved about her. And to have them bound together in soft olive skin, and expressive violet eyes with the power to heat his loins were gifts close to divine. Worthy of a god.

Her courage and beauty were rivaled by her stubbornness. Each night as he kissed and caressed her in dreams, she'd let down her guard, and take part only to deny her passion in the light of day. He'd brought her repeatedly to the pinnacle, her body writhing upon the silk, panting, screaming her release. And without breaching proof of her maidenhood. That he'd take at her insistence and when she was fully awake. Apollo glanced once more at his reflection in the mirror. He must love her to go to such lengths.

* * *

Cassie considered the woman who'd bore her and doubted the genetic connection. Her mother stood before Cassie's open closet. "Wear a dress." She plunged into the back of the walk-in depths. "Where is he taking you? Some place nice, I hope." Her mother emerged. "Wear the black number. Oh, and your diamond and sapphire earrings."

Cassie stared at her mother, holding the black lace dress above her head, shaking it in rabid insistence. "Mom, what I'm wearing is fine."

Her mother crinkled her nose and pressed the padded hanger into Cassie's hand. "Be serious. Men are visual creatures attracted to beauty." She tilted her head. "What are you doing with your hair?"

"Nothing. I like it loose."

"Then curl it."

"John likes me as I am." Cassie hoped that was true.

Her mom snickered. "Oh, the intelligent ones all say that. Every man wants a goddess on his arm. Why not oblige him?"

Patience ran short and the word *goddess* irked Cassie. "I'm not sure how I feel about John. Why should I work to impress him?"

"You're serious." Her mother's eyes widened. "You never know who you'll meet when you're out. Maybe this young man won't measure up, but another might see you across the room, be captivated by your beauty and seek you out."

Cassie couldn't believe her mom's words. Nancy Priam was a modern woman, a respected dermatologist, and way too focused on appearance. Unfortunately, not much of a surprise.

"I want to be loved for me," said Cassie, her fingers tightening on the hanger until her knuckles ached.

Her mom's shrill laugh filled the room. "A man needs a reason to invest time to know you. After he's fallen for the pretty package, you can unveil your idiosyncrasies—not before." She made a clucking sound and shook her head. "You have it so backward, dear. No wonder you young girls have trouble finding a man to marry."

Cassie flinched at the cruel remark. Her mom could be so clueless.

Dr. Nancy Priam lowered her gaze. "I'm sorry, I don't mean you, Cassie. You're too young for anything as serious as marriage. It's just that your generation is bombarded with advertising and few of you know how to market yourselves." She threw up her manicured hands. "Unbelievable."

The entire conversation was unbelievable. "I'm not a product for sale."

Her mom's red lips tightened. "It isn't a question of whether we're for sale or not. It's haggling over the price."

The shock of her mother's words shot through

Cassie like Greek fire. Did her mom believe what she'd said? In what way had Dr. Nancy Priam sold herself and to whom? Cassie took in her mom's shaking hand as it again pushed the black dress at her, the harsh lines around her mouth and desperation darkening her blue gaze. Her mom could be the poster child for misery. For the first time in Cassie's memory she felt sorry for her.

* * *

Sawdust and peanut shells were strewn about the floor of the Cattle Rustler's Bar and Eatery. Cassie followed John through the conglomerate of truckers, family parties and servers, burdened by trays stacked high, to their table in the corner. She slid into the brown vinyl-covered booth. A beer bottle dangled above the table with a bulb screwed into the cut bottom, creating a crude lamp that glowed indifferent light.

John grinned at her and pulled a peanut from the tin bucket on the table, cracking the shell in his large bronze hand. "Great place. Best steaks and ribs." He popped the nuts into his mouth and chewed. "Hope you're hungry."

The server, a thin young man decked in a black t-shirt with the words "Cattle Rustlers do it better" in beefy script over his chest, handed them menus. Cassie squinted at the offerings under the dim beer bottle and was glad she'd ignored her mom and worn jeans.

"We'll have two beers and the Stampede

Platter," said John.

"And what dressings for your salads?" The server focused on her with quick green eyes.

"Ranch on the side," she said, irritated that John had side stepped her in ordering. "And no beer, just water." The server nodded and left.

"You don't drink?" John crinkled his brow. "I knew you were brilliant. Are you a prodigy, one of those kids that finished college by sixteen? I've never been good at guessing a woman's age. You are legal—right?"

Cassie considered giving him a hard time and let him think he was out with jailbait. Served him right. He deserved to sweat it out for a while "That depends on what you mean by legal."

His gaze focused into a leveling stare. "You're full of crap."

"Am I?"

"Yeah." He drummed his fingers on the glossy wood table. "I'm an information geek. You're over 21 and no boyfriend. I checked you out before I took you to lunch."

"Okay. Now I'm uncomfortable." And his reference to "boyfriend" caused her to wonder if Apollo would barge in. Not that he was her boyfriend, but he didn't seem to listen to her on that point. She casually glanced around the room for blue eyes emitting fire.

"Why? Everyone does it. I'm just honest about it." That lopsided grin spread over his mouth. "Like you didn't look me up before tonight?"

"Maybe a little." He did have a point. "How much digging did you do?"

"Enough to know that you're a quiet girl, a serious student, and someone I'd like to know better."

All true. But she was still annoyed by his need for control. "Do you always order for your dates without asking them? And what is the *Stampede*?"

John tossed peanut shells onto the floor. "Just habit on the order. The Stampede is a platter stacked high with ribs, grilled steak and chicken. I'm a carnivore."

Habit? Did he bring a lot of girls here? Good thing she wasn't a vegetarian, she'd starve with this guy. Cassie dropped her paper napkin in her lap feeling irritation roll in her gut. "Do you frequent this place?"

John shrugged. "It's close to my apartment and I like the décor. Very low key."

Low key didn't begin to describe the design. Cassie glanced at the stuffed two-headed calf displayed on the far wall and shuddered. "It's unique."

"I thought you'd like it." John grinned and crumbled peanut shells between his fingers, littering the table with fine dust. "You're not like other girls."

She felt another of his flirtatious *lines* coming on. It was flattering that he bothered, but she preferred honesty and a direct approach. "How am I different?"

"I'm not sure, but there's something about you." He tossed a shelled nut into his mouth. "You're sweet, for one thing, and you know how to dress for a first date. None of that fancy outfit 'I'm trying to impress you' garbage. Jeans say 'take me as I am'. I like that."

What a dichotomy, an ambitious man that avoided pretension. "I didn't realize I was making a statement." She scanned John's green marine t-shirt. His tan biceps bulged beneath the short sleeves. "What are you saying with your shirt, that you're an ex-marine?"

His lips widened to that lopsided grin. "Nope. That I need to do laundry."

Cassie couldn't help but smile. John's teasing fed her need to play. It had been far too long since she'd relaxed with a man and had a good time. Who said it had to become a *relationship*?

The server brought their salads and the band started up.

"These guys are perfect," said John. "What they lack in talent they make up for in volume."

"You like them?"

"Sure." The twang of country guitar reverberated from the small stage.

"What?" This wouldn't work. "I can't hear you," she mouthed.

John snatched his plate, left his side of the booth, and scooted in beside her. "How's this?"

His hot breath tickled her ear, sending shivers down to her toes. John was cute, fun, and a lifeline to normal. She nodded, afraid her voice would squeak a reply. His clean scent wrapped around her like a warm towel fresh from the drier. Breathing in, she filled her lungs with him and memorized the perfume of rugged man and soap. Cassie stared at his eyes, but her gaze drifted to the space between his firm jaw and straight nose. His mouth intrigued her as he spoke, but she couldn't focus on the words. Each movement of his delectable lips distracted her mind. Imagination took over and she visualized how his mouth would feel on hers. Would his kiss be soft or firm and demanding?

"Well?" John stared at her, apparently expecting an answer.

Damn. In her stupor she'd missed everything he'd said. Heat crept up her neck. "Say again?"

He blew out a frustrated breath. "You didn't hear anything I said, did you? My bad. The music is too loud. If it's okay with you, we can get the food to go and enjoy a quiet dinner at my apartment."

He had her full attention. "Your place?" Imaginings of his soft lips pressing hers, crowded her mind. She swallowed. Visions of his strong arms around her and that longed for moment when he took her to his bed. Damn, she was doing it again. Focus. Hadn't she been hurt enough by men? Did she have to act like an out of control teenager? Get a grip.

She shouldn't consider a relationship with

John. Somehow she'd drive him away just as she'd done with every other guy. He'd leave her with a fresh, gaping wound to her self-esteem. Did she have a talent for picking men unable to commit? Not a pleasant thought. And there was that red flag, his need to make connections. He'd denied that his objective was to meet her dad, but she'd been lied to before. Eric had lied. Or could her mom be right, and men wanted a goddess that looked like sex on stilettos rather than someone real to build a life with? Her stomach sank. She hoped not.

Cassie took a long look at Mr. Hottie. He was ambitious. Ambition didn't guarantee that he wasn't interested in her. What if John was different from the men in her past? She could give him a chance. If he were still around in another month, she could sum up her feelings and see if a relationship added up. For the time being, her bruised ego could use some male attention from a normal guy. She scanned left and right and listened for that domineering god to object. Nothing. Not so much as a whisper. She let out a breath in relief. "Going to your apartment is a great idea."

CHAPTER EIGHT

Apollo unbuttoned his navy jacket and scanned the restaurant for Cassandra, wincing when a man on stage bellowed lyrics to a depressing tune. Did this noise pass for music in this new age? He didn't care for it. Too loud. It lacked the serene appeal of the lyre or the jovial lilt of flute and drum. His ears throbbed. Oh, that Zeus would allow him to remove offensive mortals, and then the musicians' assault would end. Still, a god had some options. Apollo glared at the man as he tortured another song. The mortal coughed, gasped and fell silent. *Ah, peace.* Rendering the players mute for an hour would do no harm.

Scanning the space, the debris on the ground made him wonder if they kept livestock within. The shreds on the ground didn't look like straw and no offensive animal odors filled his nostrils. Apollo smelled beer and charred meat, and underneath it all, the soft scent of almond oil. He honed in on the tantalizing fragrance, knowing it must belong to his wayward Cassandra. He rolled his shoulders and strode toward the compelling aroma. He spied her. Cassandra's lovely mouth formed an "oh". Apollo licked his lips. *Such a mouth needed kissing and so many other activities.*

His reverie was short-lived. The rodent sat beside her, his head dipped close to her ear as if whispering seductive words. Every muscle in Apollo's body tightened. He'd never felt such irritation. There had to be flames shooting from his eyes. Cassandra's violet orbs widened and she slid back from the offender. Wise girl. Those who angered a god could be struck by lightning.

He'd been shackled against smiting the man, but Cassandra didn't know it, and he'd use her fear of his retaliation to end her dalliance with the creature. He'd order the man away and then he'd make Cassandra listen to him, as Artemis had suggested.

Apollo strode toward the table, determined to act above the frustration gnawing at his insides. He planted himself before them, legs spread and his hands on his hips. "There you are."

The man turned and raised his brows in question. "And who are you?"

How dare this creature address him with such casual disrespect. *Impudent excuse for mortal flesh.* Heat surged through Apollo's limbs. With a bit of focus, he could singe the weasel's hair, or what remained of it. Apollo directed his remarks to Cassandra. "It's time to leave."

The rodent stood and glared at Apollo. "Look,

the lady is with me. Got it?"

Cassandra tugged at the man's arm and peaked around his side. Her eyes flashed from violet to dark purple. "What are you doing here?"

The lump of flesh glanced at her. "You know this guy?"

"Not by choice." She glared at Apollo.

"Oh." The insect hardened his stare on Apollo. "You're the loser that can't take no for an answer. Get lost, Goldilocks. She's not interested."

As a boy, Apollo had watched in disgust as Hades had pulled the legs from marsh flies for sport. As a rule, he didn't agree with torturing lesser creatures, but in this instance the practice carried some appeal. Unfortunately, Zeus wouldn't agree. Apollo refused to acknowledge the gnat. "Cassandra, we discussed this."

"There was no discussion. You decreed, like you always do." She shot arrows at him with her eyes. "Don't tell me what to do."

The man puffed up his chest. "Are you leaving or do we need to take this outside?"

With a glare, Apollo could burn the man's skin: with focus he might scar him, blind him, or castrate the dog. The creature deserved it. By all the gods, he couldn't put up with much more of this. "Mortal, you try my patience."

"Cassie wasn't kidding." The rodent smirked. "You really *do* have a god complex."

"Enough," he growled. "No puny mortal dares to speak to me thus and live." Apollo ground his teeth to curb the curse forming on his lips. He'd sworn to Zeus, but…

* * *

John swayed and fell back, wedging Cassie into the booth. His brown eyes were glassy as marbles. She pressed her fingers against his neck and checked for a pulse: strong and regular. Good. He might be okay, or at least she hoped so. Her relief for John's welfare argued with her anger. "What's wrong with you?"

Apollo cocked his head. "Me? It's impossible for anything to be wrong with me. I'm a god."

"Oh please." Cassie rolled her eyes at him. "Trust me, there's room for improvement." She strained to push John into an upright position. "You could help," she grumbled.

The god waved his hand and John sat up, faced forward and then stared sightless at the opposing seat. Apollo perused the man and made a derisive grunting noise.

Cassie narrowed her gaze at Apollo as he took the seat opposite her. "Make John as he was."

"Calm yourself. There's no harm to him. I'll waken him after you listen to me."

"The only thing I want to hear is the sound of your shoes scuffing the floor on your way out. Make it fast."

His lips pinched together. "You belong to me. It's time you accepted your position as my consort and stopped debasing yourself with this man."

"How dare you," she breathed. "I belong to no one and I'm not your plaything."

He smiled.

Was he even listening or was he mocking her? "You'll change your mind," he said.

Mocking. "The hell I will. I'll never change my mind. You're a spoiled child that abuses power. Look at what you've done to John." She pointed at his rigid body and the drool escaping the corner of his mouth. "Why on earth would I choose to be with you?"

He chuckled, infuriating her more. Apollo had used his exceptional good looks and the kisses shared in her dreams to manipulate her. That was over. "Don't laugh at me."

"You were serious?"

"Ugh. Don't I look serious?"

He focused his blue gaze on her face and nodded. "I thought you wanted to make a game of winning you."

"Game," she said overly loud, and noticed inquisitive looks leveled in their direction. She lowered her voice. "This is my life. God or not, I'm the one deciding how I live it, and it's not as your consort or girlfriend."

His usual glow dimmed along with his arrogant attitude. "And my suit?"

"What about it?"

"I wore it for you." His brows raised and he wore a hopeful puppy dog look.

She breathed in the smell of smoky barbecue

combined with honeyed Apollo and exhaled slowly. He was making an effort to win her. She might find it sweet if he hadn't turned her life upside down and changed John into a zombie. Why did Apollo have to look at her that way, all sincere and contrite, with piercing azure eyes that melted her resolve and cooled her anger? *Damn.* "The suit is very nice."

He reached across the table and took her hand. His gentle touch warmed her skin. "I care for you, Cassandra."

Her mouth went dry. Apollo was wrong for her on so many levels. How could she entertain the desire coursing through her veins? Had she cared for him before in that other life? A tremor ran up her spine. Was that fear or affirmation? No. She refused to think it. Apollo was beyond difficult and she had an embassy to save and then get back to the real world and her life. "Return John as he was."

"Why? I prefer him like this."

"I don't." She glanced at Apollo's large hand covering hers, his thumb lightly feathered over her palm, sending tingles up her arm. *Stop it and focus.* "John is a normal guy. We're having a normal dinner. It's what people do. Don't interfere."

"I have no intention of interfering where the prophecy is concerned, but this mortal... look at him." Apollo ran his gaze over John and shook his head. "He's beneath you. Only a weak mind is so easily controlled."

"Stop it." She spit the words. "I've had enough of your controlling ways. I've had enough of people's control, period. I called my dad and warned him. What more can I do? I can't make him believe me or force him to act." She scowled. "Dad's calling me tomorrow and then I'm done with it."

The muscles in his jaw worked. "Not so. This is only the beginning. My gift lasts your lifetime."

She gasped. "I didn't agree to that. You trapped me."

"I saved you."

"Ha. You'd say anything to get your way."

"I know the future. Assisting mortals against destruction is what the gods of Olympus strive for. It's the decree of Zeus, as long as we don't act ourselves in the affairs of men."

"And what do you call this?" She nodded toward John. "And what about my life? You've acted plenty. I have yet to see you use self control."

Apollo ran his tongue over his upper lip in a slow swipe that curled her toes. "Cassandra, without restraint, I'd reduce this mortal to a grease stain beneath my shoe and teach you the delights of my bed."

Heat radiated from Cassie's face and she swallowed. If she were open to unbridled sex without the promise of anything more, then Apollo might be her man, but she wasn't. Fantasy was one thing, but in real life she insisted on having a committed relationship. Gods didn't commit to mortals and Apollo was a god. He'd leave her sooner or later and she'd had enough of that. "Fine. You have a smidgen of restraint. Now, what can you do to protect the embassy?"

"I've done it. You have inspiration to guide you."

"That's it?" Cassie pulled her hand from Apollo's grasp. "What good is a god if he can't help?"

He tugged at his shirt collar and narrowed his gaze. "I can guide you to the truth and show you the future. Men have paid a high price for this knowledge. "

"Can you change what will happen?"

"That power belongs to men."

"Ugh. So you can't do anything." Her body trembled with anger. She'd like to slap him for putting her in this position. "You rotten SOB. Find someone else to save the embassy, because I'm done."

Apollo's pale gaze darkened. "You test me. Part of my agreement for your release from the underworld was your being my prophetess. There can be no other. Zeus himself agreed to the terms."

"Did I ask to be released?"

"You wept in misery." He lowered his eyes as if he dare not look at her.

"I'm sure *Cassandra* cried her eyes out in the

underworld after Troy fell, and she was raped and murdered, but I'm betting she got over it after three thousand years."

"You never 'got over it' as you call it. Your suffering played before me until I had to act."

"Stop," Cassie grumbled, and rested her head in her hands. Her ebony tresses fell over her face like a black curtain. "I don't want to hear anymore."

She might end the conversation, but ancient history mingled with her dreams and played in her mind. Horror after horror until Cassandra's murder—no—*my murder.* A tear escaped her eye and ran beside her nose. She lifted her head and focused her bleary gaze on Apollo. "Tell me one thing. Will the embassy fall?"

* * *

A strange sensation squeezed his heart. Watching her pain added to his growing discomfort. He'd felt for humanity's suffering on occasion, but none had affected him more than Cassie's single tear.

She'd received his gift. And like his ancient Cassandra, Cassie couldn't avoid its violent intrusion into her life. But he could prepare her for it.

"You've seen the attack?"

Cassie nodded and swiped at her nose with a paper napkin. "Not everything. It fades before the outcome."

Even with her red eyes and nose, she captivated him. Apollo reached out and laid his hand on her wrist. "There's a reason you didn't experience the end. It means the prophecy might be altered."

"Altered? But how?" she sniffed.

"When the vision takes you, what happens?"

She pursed her lips. "I'm part of the action and experience every terrifying moment."

John teetered and fell forward, his head thudding on the table. She gave Apollo a frigid stare. "Well?"

He breathed out in frustration. "He's fine as he is."

She crossed her arms over her chest. "I'm not *fine* with it."

Apollo glanced at John and he again sat up. His forehead showed a large red mark. Apollo crinkled his brow. "He's going to have a headache." He fished ice from the water glass, wrapped it in a napkin and handed it to Cassie. "For the bruise."

"Thanks." Cassie took the cold wad of napkins and pressed them to the red spot.

Apollo continued. "Stand back from the vision. Living it is optional."

Her violet eyes widened. "It's possible to watch and not be overcome by it all?"

"Yes. Remember the skills I taught you in the past."

"You mean Cassandra."

"You *are* Cassandra." He leveled his gaze on her. "Whether in Cassandra's body or your current temple, you have always been, and will always be the same courageous woman."

"Me courageous?" She shook her head in denial. "I'm a math nerd living at home to please my dad and wearing clothes my mother insists on so I make the right statement. And I don't know if I like any of it. I'm a coward."

"I've seen glimpses of the exceptional woman hidden beneath this beautiful surface."

Her eyes lowered from his face and focused on the table. "I'm great at languages, numbers and logic. If you need someone to balance your accounts, I'm your girl, but this situation is beyond me."

"You doubt my word. Lies hide in darkness. I'm the god of prophecy, music, light and truth. No shadow exists in me."

She focused on him, her brows lowered in what appeared effort to comprehend his words. "I don't recall your *ever* being called the deity of truth. Are you lying to me now?"

"I *don't* lie. There's a difference."

"And what would happen if you did?"

"I would cease to be who I am."

Cassie's mouth curved down. "Maybe I'm not the same person you believe me to be. Is it possible that any courage I had was snuffed out along with Cassandra's life? You said that I never got over it."

"Your heart hasn't changed, my love." His blue eyes turned azure as his face softened. "Compassion drove you in the past, as it does now. You've subjected yourself to your father and mother out of love. Your desire to save people you don't know is motivated from the same force. To sacrifice for another requires the greatest courage."

"Sacrifice, huh. Is it too much to ask that I don't replay all of Cassandra's life?" She urged her mouth into a tremulous smile. "From what I remember, I didn't enjoy that at all."

CHAPTER NINE

John blinked into consciousness. "I have such a headache. If you don't mind, I can get our order to go."

Cassie backtracked to the end of their conversation before Apollo had made him a zombie. "Oh yes, we were headed to your apartment." Apparently Apollo had wiped John's memory before he left. A good thing too, she didn't want to have to explain the last hour or her odd relationship to a god. "Food to go would be fine, but do you feel all right? Maybe you should rest. I can take a cab home."

John squinted at her. "I'll be okay after a few aspirin and some quiet."

"If you're sure?" She stared at the bruise forming on his head.

"I'm feeling better every minute."

* * *

Cassie sat in John's apartment: white walls, beige carpet and red couch. The red fit his bold personality. The leftover pizza and dirty glasses on the coffee table, combined with his boxers flung over a recliner, led her to suspect that Mr. Hunky Buzzcut didn't live the average, well-ordered life of a computer geek and wanna be FBI agent.

There was another side to this man. She ran her hand behind the cushion pressed into her back and yanked out a half-eaten grilled cheese sandwich. *Gross.* She dropped the greasy crust onto the stale pizza. Dull, average and set in routine didn't appeal to her, but this was disgusting.

He returned with their drinks. "Sorry, no clean glasses." John handed her a can of cola. "I'm reheating our food, it'll only take a minute."

"Thanks." Her gaze fixed on his eyes. No longer frozen as a dolls, but full of life. Would there be long-term effects from his stint as a zombie? She squeezed the frigid can, her fingers chilling. *Damn Apollo.*

She focused on the goose egg growing above John's right eye as he sat beside her. He had to feel it. "How's your head?"

"Much better." He put his soda can on the table. Moisture beaded on the cold surface and trickled onto the dusty coffee table. Cassie quelled the urge to wipe away the grime and the water pooling around the can's base. John rubbed his hand on the leg of his jeans, looking at her with interest. "I can't believe you're single. Has your dad scared off men or are they all just blind and stupid?"

The last thing she wanted to discuss was her romantic past. "Something like that." She stared at the can as another bead of moisture ran onto the table.

He nodded. "Oh, the last break-up is still raw. I get it. My heart's been ripped out a few times."

"You?" Cassie felt her eyes bulge in disbelief. John Medina didn't look or act like a man who had trouble with women. More likely they had trouble with him. He was too charming and sexy for a computer nerd. Most of those guys felt safe. Perched on John's couch, Cassie wondered if he'd break her heart.

"Yep," he sighed. "Maybe I'm too honest. I don't know."

"Honest or blunt?"

He lowered his dark brows. "Women say they want honesty, but that's a lie. Most want a fairytale. I'm not that man. I live in the real world. I see what I want and go after it without apology. No pretending about it." He ran his tongue along his upper lip. "Yeah, I don't believe in wasting time playing games."

Cassie didn't know what to say. She hadn't lived one hundred percent in the real world since Greece. But she wanted to. "Fantasy is overrated and a little goes a long way."

"You're not just blowing smoke up my ass?" He leaned toward her, crowding her space.

She smelled the clean scent of him. Cassie

leaned back, but found the firm arm of the couch barring her retreat. "I was raised with logic and real."

"I bet you were. When I first saw you, I thought you looked like a no-nonsense type. No games, just get down to it, be honest and tell it like it is." His tongue made another swipe over his lip. "If I ask you something, will you tell me the truth?"

The back of Cassie's neck tingled and her stomach knotted. "I guess." Was this date with John a bad idea?

"Why did you agree to go out with me?"

"I liked you."

His lopsided grin formed. "And why did you want to come to my apartment?"

"I, um. The restaurant was noisy and you had a headache." Had she made a mistake in coming here?

He leaned back against the couch and looked her up and down. "I see."

Her neck prickled something fierce. Cassie recognized the danger signal, but didn't know how to react. "See what?"

"Your story is a load of crap," he said, and shifted closer to her. His brown eyes turned smoky. "If you wanted us to be alone, all you had to do was say so." He slid his brawny arm around her and pulled her against him. "It's always the serious ones."

Her mouth went dry and her heart slammed

against her ribs. "You have the wrong idea. I wanted…"

He cut her off. "And I'm gonna give it to you, baby." His lopsided grin widened, but this time it didn't release butterflies, it turned her stomach. "I can get into role-play if you want. I'll be the big, strong government agent and you can be the enemy spy or a very naughty double agent in need of debriefing." He wrapped his arms around her like a python.

"Let me loose." Cassie shoved against him to little effect. "You bastard."

He pushed her down on the lumpy couch and straddled her. "You want it a little rough? I like that. I have handcuffs." He grabbed her wrists in one hand, yanked them over her head and retrieved the silver cuffs from his back pocket.

"No! I don't want *it* at all. Get the hell off me," she spit and twisted her body, but he pressed his weight on her. She couldn't move. This couldn't be happening.

"Oh you want it, you little tease," he said against her ear, and then shackled her wrists. He shoved his knee between her legs, spreading them. "You've been after me to give it to you since we met."

She quivered. Her lungs seized. Blood pounded in her temples. Cassie struggled beneath his hulking mass. "Let. Me. Go," she ground out between breaths.

"You're good at this." He laughed. "You've

done this before." He released the top button of her jeans.

"Apollo," she shrieked. "Help."

John clamped a meaty hand over her mouth. "Hey, I have neighbors. I like realism, but keep it down."

Desperate, Cassie opened her mouth to bite the fingers stealing her breath.

"Ouch." John pulled his hand from her lips and shoved a dirty sock between her teeth. "Go ahead, sweet meat, yell all you want."

"Apollo," Cassie grunted around the sock, and did her best to keep from retching and choking herself.

A flash of light.

One moment John's weight crushed her, and the next his body was suspended flat against the ceiling. His eyes were wild orbs of fear, brown dots surrounded by bulging white, and his mouth did an excellent impression of a gasping trout.

Apollo shimmered with golden light as he stretched his arm in the direction of John. His fingers opened and closed in tight undulating action. John groaned with each fisted move from the angry god's hand. White-hot lasers streamed from Apollo's narrowed glare. The brown buzz smoldered, smoke wafted from the stubble on the sides of John's head, and a blue flame danced over the tops of the fuzzy edges of his cropped hair. It sizzled. The scene reminded her of a marshmallow on a stick too close to the campfire. His hair glowed with heat. Apollo blew out a breath and snuffed the flame, leaving black soot in place of the buzzed strands. It was not a good look for him. John went limp. A glassy stare replaced his horrified gape.

Apollo strode to Cassie's side and pulled the sock from her mouth. She grimaced and spit to cast off the taste of bad cheese. Her frame trembled from adrenaline and relief. "I've never been so happy to see anyone in my life."

* * *

Apollo released her chains, lifted her off the couch and hugged her close. He quaked inside from fear of what might have befallen her. She flung her arms around his neck. Her slender shoulders shook from sobs wrenched from her gut. Choked breaths struggled between each wail. Tears flooded her eyes and moistened the top of his toga. Apollo hated seeing her in such anguish. It brought him back to Troy and all the torment she'd suffered. And again, the fault lay with him.

"Hush now," he whispered over her dark hair. "I have you." He took her away to a place of safety, the olive grove from her dreams.

Cassie snuggled against his chest and hiccupped a breath. "This place is real? I thought it was in my head." Tremors continued to shake her until her tears were spent and she rested in his arms. "I'm sorry for being so stupid," she mumbled into his robe. "I guess I should have known better than to come to John's apartment."

"You're naive about men. It's not your fault. You have little experience."

She tilted her face up to him. Her eyes were red and swollen, and her skin blotched pink. "I'm old enough to have a brain," she sniffed. "I've never had this problem. The men I've gone out with never tried anything. Maybe they were afraid of my dad. I don't know. None of them stuck around." She dabbed at her eyes with the gold embroidered edge of his cloak. "I just figured that I wasn't attractive."

He hugged her to his heart where he wanted to keep her safe. "That wasn't it."

Cassie stilled. Her gaze darkened from violet to purple. "You know something about this. Why has every man dumped me as if I had snakes crawling on my head, like I was cursed or something?"

"I..." He glanced up at a sparrow perched on a branch. Apollo hoped she'd appreciate the truth.

"Did you do something?" She scrunched her mouth together as if she'd sucked vinegar.

"It was for your protection."

"What was?" She leaned back from him. "Did you curse me and make me disgusting to men?"

He'd tell her the truth, though for once he didn't want to. "I'd never curse you, beloved."

"But you did something?" She stared at him with accusation deep in her red-rimmed eyes.

"They were wrong for you. The first young

man only wanted your body and you couldn't see it. He would have used you. And that high school boy, he thought only of himself."

"Oh, and you don't?" She thumped him on the chest with her fist. "Did you ruin every relationship?"

"No. They weren't relationships."

"Ugh!" She squirmed in his arms and he let her go "You made sure of that," she huffed.

"I made sure you wouldn't be hurt."

She swung her arm back and slapped his face. He barely felt it, but she cradled her hand and jumped around. "Ouch, ouch, ouch." She glared at him. "Damn you. That hurt."

He shrugged. "And you're surprised by this?"

Cassie manipulated her wrist and rotated her hand, checking its condition. "I shouldn't be surprised by anything you do." She clenched her fingers as if considering another go at him. "I thought you were forbidden to interfere in the lives of men. What gave you the right to ruin mine?"

"Right? You belong to me. I knew what those men were. They couldn't love you." He breathed through annoyance. How could she accuse him? Didn't she understand the danger those mortals posed to her? "Look at the singed rat hanging above. If I hadn't appeared when I did, you'd be more than hurt. I've always protected you from creatures like that loathsome rodent."

Her body stood rigid, her hands wrapped into

tight fists at her sides. He waited for her to rail against him. "Send me back right now," she spoke through tight lips.

"To that insect's apartment?" Had the incident clouded her mind?

"Don't be ridiculous. Outside will be fine."

Apollo chose to let her go to cool down. He waved his hand and granted her request. Perhaps she wanted revenge on the creature.

Then he appeared inside John's apartment and glanced at Medina hanging on the ceiling. The acrid smell from burned hair filtered over the room. Apollo considered taking out his anger on the man by chaining him to a mountainside for the birds to feast upon, but no matter how deserving this mortal was of punishment, Zeus forbade it.

The god raised his hand and the man fell to the ground like an over ripe fig. The mortal grunted, rolled over and blinked at Apollo. "What happened?"

Apollo stood over the puny mortal and denied the urge to make him a eunuch. "If you touch Cassie again, by Zeus, I'll flay your hide."

CHAPTER TEN

The otherworld of the gods had been Apollo's retreat from humanity for thousands of years. It had been the haven he'd sought after Troy. Today, it held only irritation and dread. Zeus commanded his presence.

The abode of his father had changed over millennia. Going from the classical design of marble columns to baroque carved woods, and extravagant silk brocade, and back again. This current decoration included all that Zeus enjoyed from both. His father called it an eclectic mix of mortal talents. Apollo didn't care for it, but he wasn't fool enough to voice his opinion.

Apollo dressed in his robes and approached Zeus in the garden. His father clad in shorts, a t-shirt, and some rubberized covering on his feet. Zeus scowled at a sapling avocado tree.

"Still working on the problem of the size of the pit?" Apollo asked in casual conversation. Zeus spent eternities perfecting nature and it irked his wife, Hera. That was her realm.

"I've gotten the pit smaller, but the flavor of

the fruit is hampered." He held an avocado in his hand and turned it over with his agile fingers. "The balance is all wrong, but I'll make it right."

His father insisted on all creation following his commands, from the smallest water bug to the gods, and those that refused were dealt with. Apollo's stomach knotted with apprehension. "You called for me?"

Zeus focused his sea-green gaze on him and Apollo saw a storm brewing in their depths. "I've been watching you," said Zeus.

Apollo shrugged. His father might have a task for him or a reprimand. He'd wait and see before he spoke.

"You've come dangerously close to breaking my laws."

Reprimand. "I didn't smite the rodent or move him to another location, only hung him from a ceiling for a short time."

"And what excuse do you give for cursing the man in public? People saw his catatonic state. And the guitar player? I understand that he lacked talent, but you acted before a room full of mortals."

Apollo clenched his jaw to curb his tart reply. Best to ask forgiveness when his father was in a volatile mood. "It won't happen again."

"It had better not. Hades is eyeing you and reports all your misdeeds abroad. He wants to win your wager."

"He won't win."

"Are you so sure? I watched your disaster with Cassandra. You admitted to interfering in her personal life. Another violation." Tension edged his voice.

"Did you want me to lie?"

"I wanted you to keep the law and not dabble in mortal choice." Zeus rumbled and squeezed the avocado until the soft green flesh escaped between his fingers. "You continue to ignore my decrees and I won't have it."

Apollo lowered to his knees and bowed his head. "Forgive me."

"Forgive? With Hades proclaiming your defiance among the gods, I *must* punish you."

"As you will." Apollo's stomach turned over on itself. Zeus was legendary for handing out creative punishments. Apollo lifted his head and dared to look at his father, hoping for his mercy but not sure his mood would grant it.

"And you best remember that." Zeus cleansed the oily fruit from his hand in a shimmer of gold and stared at Apollo. His gaze softened from turbulent green to cool blue.

It gave Apollo courage. "Give me another chance. I will abide by your laws."

"I must punish you, but I will be merciful— this time."

"Thank you for your mercy, father." Mercy from Zeus could be torture. Sweat moistened Apollo's skin as he awaited the decree.

* * *

Cassie paced outside of John's apartment on the sidewalk, waiting for a cab. The scent of him stuck to her clothes and she wanted to gag. She fumed with rage. Every muscle in her body ached from fighting Mr. Horny. She was angry with John for being a pervert, angry with Apollo for doing something to run off every man she'd ever wanted a relationship with, but, most of all, she was furious with herself for trusting either one of them.

For being a smart girl, she sure felt dumb. Why hadn't she asked Apollo to drop her off in her room at home? She wanted to scream. Adrenaline made her legs quake and she forced herself to pace faster. At least she'd stopped her tears. Good thing she hadn't worn the dress her mom had pushed at her. That would have made it too easy for the perv. She made a mental note: In the future, always wear snug jeans on a first date. *Like I'm ever going out again, huh.*

The cab pulled up. Cassie got in and used the drive home to repair her appearance. Her hair was a mess and she smoothed her hands over it to calm her bird's-nest tresses. The hem of her blouse was torn and the top button was gone. She must look like a girl who'd taken a tumble in bed. Her mother would give her a talking to when she hit the door and Cassie did not want to have that conversation.

She breathed through another surge of anger. She'd get Medina banned from the FBI and tossed out of school. He should be locked up, but her father didn't need his daughter's face pasted all over the tabloids crying rape. And who would believe her? Assault maybe, but the papers would enjoy that almost as much. No. She'd tell her dad, John would lose his dream, and she hoped that would teach him a lesson.

Dad. Reality hit her in the face like a fist. He would think she'd lost it. His princess, with no long-term relationships, no men interested in her at all, and now after Eric had devastated her, crying assault on the next guy willing to give her a look. She punched the back of the car's seat. "Damnit! He'll have me evaluated for sure."

The driver shook his head, but kept driving.

"Whatever," she grumbled. Cassie couldn't take time to worry about what the cab driver thought of her. There were bigger issues. Apollo had added to her trouble. If it hadn't been for him scaring off men all her dating life, she might have learned enough to see John for the disgusting sex fiend that he was. She might even be happily in a relationship, and not tempted by a hunky guy with one thing on his mind.

And then for Apollo to justify his actions by saying he knew best and was protecting her. What she needed was protection from him. Who did he think he was, a god? Nervous giggles erupted from her lips. "A god," she snorted. The driver glanced in his rearview mirror and drove faster. Hysterics continued the rest of the way home.

Cassie paid the driver and swiped at her wet eyes. It was early. She hoped she could bypass her mom and sneak unseen upstairs to her room. Tiptoeing around the back of the house, she opened the kitchen door. It was past dinnertime and her parents ate most meals out. No one would see her.

She held her breath and opened the door. The kitchen was dark. Good. Cassie slipped off her pumps and padded over the ceramic tile towards the back stairs leading up to the hall near her room. She lifted her foot and landed on something lumpy. A screech echoed up the stairs and through the house. A large gray mass shot by her. Cassie joined in with her own surprised scream, followed by another fit of laughter.

"Damn cat." she snorted, and giggled until her sides ached.

The lights glared on. "Cassie?"

Cassie's snickering faded. "Hi, Mom. I just stepped on Ajax. Sorry."

Her mom's face was hidden behind a mask of blue algae. It cracked when her mouth twisted and her eyes bugged out. "What happened to you?"

"Mom, I don't want to discuss it." Cassie sagged against the kitchen cabinets.

"Are you hurt?" Her mom scanned her from across the kitchen and the safety of the light switch.

"My blouse has seen better days."

"That's not what I meant."

"I'm fine." Cassie turned toward the back stairs.

"Are you drunk?"

Cassie faced her mother. "What?"

"I said, are you drunk? I hope you didn't make a scene at the restaurant with that man you went out with."

Fire blasted through Cassie's limbs and shot through her mouth in the form of words. A torrent of Greek, Italian, German and French colorful language directed at her clueless and self-absorbed mother. After the verbal assault, Cassie gritted her teeth and spoke in English. "Is that what you're worried about? You're afraid I might have been seen and embarrassed you?"

"Were you?" Her mother glared at her.

"Yes, Mom. I drank myself silly, danced on tabletops and sang 101 Bottles of Beer on the Wall at the top of my lungs. Then I found some random guy and had sex with him on the hood of his rusty pick-up truck in the parking lot. It was quite a show."

Dr. Nancy gaped in horror and her blue mask flaked, showing patches of pale skin beneath. "You did no such thing."

Cassie lifted her chin. "No Mom, I did no such thing, but maybe I should have."

"Don't talk like that." Her mom clutched the tie of her white terrycloth robe. "Hush," she hissed. "The household staff is here. Someone might be listening."

"You're right. I'm sure *someone* is." That overbearing god was no doubt eavesdropping. *Jerk.* Cassie bent down, slipped into her pumps and headed to the door. She couldn't stay there another moment.

"Where do you think you're going?" Dr. Nancy's shrill tone challenged.

"Out dancing."

* * *

It felt like an eternity as Apollo waited for Zeus to announce his punishment. It could be an impossible series of tasks or a stint in another form like a crow. Either of those would ensure his loss of the wager. Losing against Hades would be punishment enough.

Apollo played his lyre to calm his nerves and urge his father into a more gracious temper. After his fifth tune, Zeus spoke. "I've made my decision. I strip you of your gift of prophecy. If you bear your punishment well, and do as I command, I will reinstate the gift."

"When will it return?" This was lenient for Zeus, but he knew it would end the gift he'd given Cassie and her ability to save the embassy.

Zeus looked down his nose at him. "In a century or two or when the mood strikes me."

Apollo struggled not to argue and accept the decree, but with Cassie's life and the mortals in

Athens at risk, he had to challenge it. He fell again to his knees. "Choose something else. Without prophecy, the embassy will fall and Hades will win the wager."

"You should've thought of this before you acted against my laws. The punishment stands." Zeus motioned for him to get off his knees. "You might still win the bet. You're my son, a handsome god, talented, and you already know much about the attack. I'm sure you can figure a way to stop Hydra and gain Cassandra's love."

Apollo nodded. "I must."

"You will. Go now and abide by my decree." His mouth pinched tight together and the color of his eyes shifted from serene blue-gray to virulent black. "But I warn you, with the next offence you'll feel the full weight of my wrath."

Apollo knew better than to open his mouth again. Sweat beaded his brow at the thought of Zeus's rage. His father's formidable arsenal included thunderbolts. Apollo had no intention of being on the receiving end of a lightning strike. He bowed and left the garden.

Without prophecy to help him thwart Hydra, he'd have to use his other skills while obeying every minute law that Zeus had imposed on the gods. No more straddling the line. No more interceding in Cassie's life by saving her from the vultures that circled her, looking for an easy meal. That insect's attack should've put fear into her. She'd be careful. Relationships with men would be the farthest thing from her mind. She was probably home right now fast asleep in her little bed.

Apollo strode into the courtyard, focused on making a plan, until the rancid stench of death ran up his nose and stopped him. In the abode of the gods, only one thing carried that smell.

"Nephew." Hades ambled toward him, his black robes frayed from decomposition as the rest of him eternally rotted, but was not consumed. "I heard about your troubles and you have my sympathy."

Hades was a liar and didn't deal in sympathy. Betrayal, kidnapping and rape, yes, but not sympathy. "Uncle," Apollo grumbled. "I have no troubles, just a challenge or two, but I'll overcome."

"It's unfortunate about your prophetic gift being taken from you." Hades shook his head of stringy gray hair. The action sent the stink wafting around him. "I hope it won't affect our wager? I'd hate to win by unfair advantage."

Apollo breathed through his mouth to lessen the smell. "I have other abilities to rely on. I'll win. You can be sure of it."

"The embassy? You might be able to save Athens. I grant you that. But Cassandra." He sighed. "Poor, sweet, virginal Cassandra. I don't know how you'll gain her trust, much less her love, after violating her choice as you did."

How did his uncle know about him chasing

off her suitors? Hades had spent most of his existence in the underworld in caves amid pools of steaming earth and lava. His spectral person only came to the heavens upon Zeus's invitation. "You've heard wrong. I protected her and she'll see that in no time."

"Will she?" He closed his pale eyes and rubbed the bridge of his bony nose. "I hear that she is vexed with you."

"Where did you hear that? Or are you making it up like the nightmares you inflict on children?"

Hades smiled, showing his discolored teeth surrounded by thin pale lips. "You've relied on prophecy to know what was coming. It's a pity. You are at a disadvantage. Get yourself some minions."

"Minions?" He'd had servants, but not anyone in the pursuit of information. He'd never needed them, until now.

"The world is full of willing mortals begging to worship a god and do him service."

"I don't like all that hovering, bowing and scraping. It's demeaning to the mortal and to the god who allows such activity."

"Minions can be most useful." Hade's widening grin did nothing to improve his face.

"I'm sure they can be, but I choose against using them."

"Then I suppose you don't wish to know what mine uncovered."

"Not in the least." Apollo wanted to be off and

rid himself of this specter of a god.

"Well, it's for the best. You probably already know what Cassandra is doing."

"Of course."

"Since you're so sure, let's increase the wager. If you gain Cassandra's love and save the embassy, I will be your servant and something more. I'll give you my dog, Kerberos, that guards the gates to the underworld.

"You'd part with the three-headed beast? What do you want in return?"

"Nothing much. Just your golden head of hair. I've admired yours a long time. Before Zeus forced me to rule the underworld, I had soft blond waves like yours. It's an old man's pleasant memory. That's what I ask for."

"My hair? You mean for me to shave it like a sheep and hand it over to you in a sack like wool?"

"It will grow back."

Apollo grumbled. Not his crowning glory. He wouldn't recognize himself.

"I ask for something that you will regain in a few months. If you win, you keep my dog forever. There is no better hunter or tracker in the entire universe. You'll be able to beat Hermes in the hunt."

"Hermes?" Apollo had been at odds with his half brother ever since Hermes had stolen his cattle. The offer tempted him. "I keep your dog and you get my locks. That's it. No trickery?"

"Just as you've said."

Apollo wished he could use prophecy to see the future of this choice, but he had to rely on his own mind. It would be a prize to humble Hermes by besting him. He thought himself so swift. Apollo would show him. "I agree to your terms."

"Excellent," said his uncle. "I mustn't keep you any longer. You already know what Cassandra is doing and must be on your way.

"Doing?"

"How she runs the streets alone, distraught and vulnerable."

Was it a lie? It *did* come through the vile mouth of Hades. Still, he should find her just to be sure. Cassie had to be sleeping by this hour.

* * *

Cassie drove her Audi to the closest bar she knew. A dive by any standards and her mom would have harsher words for the place. Two husky bikers sat outside, smoking rolled cigarettes. Leather covered their bodies and studs glinted from their mouths, along with heavy chains slung over their thick necks. She slipped out of her car, locked it, and strode through the parking lot as if she belonged there. One of the bikers shot her a hot look and curled his lips before he stuck out his tongue and wiggled it in lewd invitation. "Hey babe, how much?"

How much indeed. She was no cheap whore. She wasn't even a loose woman or a gal looking for a good time. Maybe she should have fixed her hair and changed her blouse. The missing button wasn't helping her. All she wanted was a drink. A real drink, none of the girly wine cocktails or the usual rum and cola for her. Not tonight. After the day she'd had, all Cassie wanted was to get mind-numbingly drunk. She hoped it would be worth the hangover in the morning. That headache couldn't be worse than her date with John, or Apollo's declaration, or her mother's cruel and thoughtless words.

She ignored the gestures and catcalls of the bikers and strode on her pumps into the bar. The reek of beer and stale air almost set her back on her heels and into the cool night. Not happening. She meant to get a drink and she'd have one.

This grimy, dark hole was just the spot. It looked as miserable as she felt. A section near the end of the marred wooden bar called to her. Cassie slid onto a vacant stool and glanced at the paper napkins printed with low-class humor littering the length of the bar. Yuck. She breathed in and then thought better of it as a pungent guy walked by wearing a wifebeater. Maybe she'd have just one drink and then go.

"I'm Derek. What can I get you?" The voice dragged her attention to the middle-aged bartender, gray at his temples and balding on top. He had kind gray eyes.

"I'll have—" she hesitated. What did she want to drink? It's not like she had much experience with alcohol. The girls she hung out with drank a glass of wine and that was the extent of it. This place didn't look like they carried much of a wine list. A man in the next seat ordered a Long Island ice tea. Hmmm. That sounded good.

"I'll have the same." She said the words as if she drank this all the time and waited for the drink. The bar filled with bodies. The smell of sweat-dampened shirts combined with cologne and alcohol. She wouldn't have picked a place like this on a bet, but it was just what she needed. A crap bar for the crappy way she felt.

The Long Island pushed over the scarred bar top and rested before her. It was tall and looked brown like a good glass of strong iced tea. She liked iced tea. She took a sip from the thin plastic straw. The liquid burned her throat. This was more than plain earl grey. She noticed the guy sitting next to her nursing his drink. He grinned at her and winked a brown eye. She shivered. Not happening. She'd dealt with enough male sexual urges to last her a lifetime. It didn't matter to her that the guy was a little cute in his jeans and white t-shirt. His dark hair and shadow of a beard made him look dangerous, the look of a man able to give a girl a hot kiss and know how to please her. He'd be a good choice if she were into that casual hot-and-bothered kind of no-strings night of passion.

Cassie shifted her gaze to the bartender. Derek had a snub nose and a one-inch scar on his chin from when he might have taken a hit in the bad end of a fight, or just clipped it falling down on the ice some frigid night on the streets after work. Yep. He would do fine. This was a guy she could pour out her troubles to as he poured alcohol into her glass. That's what she wanted tonight, someone to talk to who wouldn't remember what she'd said or who she was in the morning. And she wouldn't recall him either. The more she drank, the more comfortable she felt. She'd stay a while.

Cassie took another long drag from the straw. She didn't notice the burn anymore, but it made her a little lightheaded. Not that that was a problem. It was just what she'd come for. To get drunk, dance on a table or two, sing and whatever came to mind, and then catch a cab and head for home. The rest of her story about the sex on the hood of a truck was scratched from her itinerary. No way was her first time having sex going to look like that.

Female laughter brought Cassie's focus to a group seated at a table behind her, six women in their mid-twenties to early thirties. Cassie wished that she were having a good time with her friends like these women. They talked and one of them screamed with joy when the girl in the short bob flashed the ring on her finger. That's what it meant to be alive in this world and to be a part of it. All she'd done was calculate figures, please her parents and date losers. That wasn't living. That was torture and slow death.

Was that why she hadn't had many relationships, and why she maintained virgin status? Had it been Apollo chasing the men off or was it her? Cassie's thoughts were cloudy. It had to be the drink. She sounded boring even to her own ears. No one thought numerical theory was interesting except another math nerd. She'd thought pervert computer geek John Medina understood and might like her. Boy, was she wrong. Apollo seemed to be the only available male who didn't yawn in her presence.

She shook her head, letting her messy hair fall to the side of her face, and draped over the bar. Damn, but if Apollo wasn't perfect for her in some ways. The truth of that irritated her. Too bad he wasn't a man.

Apollo cared for her in his way. He obviously believed that he was protecting her. Surely not every man was out to use her and needed to be scared away. No. She'd done some of that herself. Apollo had mentioned a couple of the men she'd dated, but not all. There were others, and, for whatever reason, they weren't interested. Apollo was. But did he only want what he didn't get from Cassandra? The thought of their bodies tangled together in sheets invaded her mind and warmed her skin. Those wicked dreams gave her pause. Would it be so bad to actually have sex with Apollo? It would be a memorable first time and, by the look of things, her only opportunity. There was no way she was succumbing to men like John.

A few more sips from the straw brought the sound of sucking air. She pulled out the straw and went for the dregs. It didn't taste strong to her anymore, but went down smooth like, well, like iced tea on a hot summer day. "Another, please." She waved her empty glass at Derek. He nodded.

Cassie hated to think that the one man meant for her was the arrogant and all too gorgeous Apollo, but that's how it looked. Maybe if she drank enough of that tea it would look different. She drank. "Really good tea." By the time she'd drained the glass, she had another staring back at her.

Derek smiled. "Are you doing all right, little lady?"

"Oh yeah, just fine," she mumbled. "How about you keep these tea things coming for as long as I can manage to stay on this seat."

"Are you driving?"

"Do I look like I'm driving? I'm sitting here talking to you."

He gave her a long look and then laughed. "Either you've had enough and I got to cut you off or you're one hell of a funny gal."

"That's me, life of the party. Just ask my wannabe boyfriend, the god. He'll tell you."

He laughed again. "That sounds like a story. So where is this god of a boy friend? I'd notice a guy like that in here."

"He's around. Probably making some one miserable besides me. I think that's his official job on Mount Olympus, misery maker."

"Mount Olympus? Isn't that some where near by? Sure, there's a restaurant with that name. Do you work there?"

Cassie snorted. "No. I don't work there. I'm a student and world saver. That's not my official title, but that's what I do. The gal that sees the future and stops the bad guys." She took another gulp and sloshed the contents onto the bar as she put the vessel down.

"Nope you're drunk, little girl. I have to take your drink."

"Oh come on. I'm not drunk yet."

"Believe me, you're pickled. I hope you can walk out that door. I'll call you a cab."

"Thanks Derek, but I have to do something first."

"The ladies room is straight across." He pointed. "You can't miss it."

She shrugged. She only needed a table to dance on and some music. Cassie swayed and slid from her stool. The place had cleared out some, and she spied an empty table.

"Thanks," she said, and threw down a few bills. She weaved her way through the tables and found a spot. She lifted one spiked heel onto the wooden chair, latched on to the back with her hands for balance and hoisted herself up.

A pair of arms yanked her off. Her feet suspended in mid-air. "What the hell?" She twisted her head to see who had her.

And a pair of green eyes set in the face of an angel stared back. "Not happening, babe."

She moaned. "Oh come on. Why would you care?"

"Because I work here and this is my job, to stop pretty girls from making fools of themselves. Besides, we don't need a lawsuit when you fall off of that table and break something."

"I won't break anything. I'm going to dance."

"Not in your condition. I doubt you can walk a straight line."

"I'm not after walking, just dancing."

"Oh, I can see that, how about sitting?" And the man plopped her into the wooden chair. "What is a girl like you doing here?"

"I'm getting drunk, and dancing on this table, and then I'm singing a few songs."

"And that's your plan?"

"Yes. And you're ruining it." She squinted at him. He had nice green eyes.

"Not a very good plan." His mouth pinched together as he looked her over. "You might want to sober up first."

"I wouldn't do it if I weren't drunk."

"Well you got that part down."

"I do?"

"Yes. You need to go home."

Her shoulders slumped. "Oh no I don't. I need to dance."

The man waved over a waitress. "Coffee," he called. "A pot."

Cassie blinked. "You're thirsty."

"It's for you. I don't want you passing out before we can tell the cab where to take you."

"I don't feel so well."

"Oh no you don't. You're going to the head or outside. Which is it?"

"Outside," she groaned.

He hauled her out the door.

She gulped in the cool air and her stomach rolled. She bent over and spewed ice tea all over her shoes and dribbled goo from her mouth.

"Just in time," said green eyes.

Cassie shook, swayed and staggered away from the puddle. Green eyes pulled out his phone. "Where do you live?"

She squinted to focus on him, "How do you do that? How do you make yourself all squiggly?"

He shook his head. "I need your address. What is it?"

"Just take me to Mount Olympus. I want to get with a tasty god. Yeah, that's it." She teetered. "Oh, no, better not. I'm drunk." Cassie slumped onto the black top and wiped the sticky goo off her mouth with her sleeve. "Do you want to date me?"

"Ummm." His mouth twitched. "I'm married."

"Too bad. You seem like a nice guy."

"Your address?"

"Oh yeah. I have to get home. I have school in the morning." And then the world turned black.

CHAPTER ELEVEN

Apollo hated relying on human media, but as Hades had pointed out, he'd lost his gift and he lacked minions. It was all over the news. Cassie Priam missing. Apollo found it odd that a grown woman didn't have the freedom to be abroad without all this interest. It must be her attention-seeking mother and her father's position that had brought this on. He'd viewed them both over the years and found Dr. Priam lacking honest affection.

He watched the report on the row of televisions at the electronics store. The wonders that human science had come up with astounded him. Dr. Priam tearfully recited the tale of Cassie storming out of the house. It sounded likely. Cassie had been a in a foul mood when he'd last seen her. Where would she go? He searched his memory for her private hideaway, but nothing beyond her room came to mind.

He'd find out more from her family. Apollo had worn the suit that irritated him but would be appropriate for mortal interaction. In a flash, he left the blaring televisions and stood outside her home. He rang the bell.

A dark-jacketed man answered the door. "Dr. Priam is giving interviews out back on the patio. Who are you with, Channel Five or one of the other stations?"

"Olympus," Apollo answered, only stretching the truth.

"Hmm," said the mortal, crinkling his aged brow. "That must be a new e-paper. Where's your press ID?"

Apollo smiled "All is in order."

The man nodded in vacant agreement. "Head around the side of the house and sign in." The man closed the door, ending the conversation.

Apollo followed the voices and found Dr. Priam acting the part of distraught mother, wringing her hands and sighing. "I hope nothing terrible has happened. But in this world?" She wiped her eyes. "My husband left for Greece yesterday. It's such a trial to deal with this alone."

What had happened after Cassie left him? His chest rumbled as irritation formed a growl and he swallowed it. He must calm down or he'd singe someone.

Dr. Priam was a true thespian by the look of her contorted features. She moaned in agony and bewailed her situation as the worried mother of a wayward daughter. Apollo knew the woman well and this act couldn't fool him. He very much doubted that it fooled the crowed of reporters hovering around her either. Regardless of his distaste for the woman, he had to interject himself in the mêlée and play his own part.

He used his divine abilities to walk through the crowd and pass the stiff suited, secret service agents unseen. When he opened their awareness of him, Apollo already stood beside Dr. Priam. "I came as soon as I heard." The agents moved closer, their hands slipping to their weapons beneath their coats.

"Who are you?" Surprise apparent for a split second and then gone as Dr. Priam's eyes narrowed. "Are you the man she went out with last night?" she hissed under her breath.

Apollo hadn't thought he'd be mistaken for the rodent. "No. I'm not. I haven't seen her." He didn't want to lie, but the complete truth wasn't wise. Zeus would drag him to Mount Olympus for greater punishment.

The thought of his wager with Hades sunk deep into his brain and he couldn't risk losing. Cassie trapped in Hades' abode and at his mercy curdled his gut. Serving his putrid uncle added to his discomfort. His lungs constricted and he shook his mane of golden hair. Still attached.

"We're engaged," he said. That was close to consort, not a total lie, just the bending of the truth. He could live with it. The media clambered around him, not in reverent adoration befitting a god, but like hyenas circling a carcass.

"Where did you meet her?" shouted multiple

voices. "What's your name?" vibrated from the side. Reporters pressed closer, held back by security.

Cassie's mother stared with hard speculation. "Of course. You met her in?"

"Greece," he answered. "On a trip to Delphi." At least that was true.

Her mouth spread into a tense grin. "How and when exactly did you get engaged to my daughter?"

How could he put this and be honest? He couldn't admit he'd demanded she be his consort. That wasn't the mortal equivalent to promising marriage. Marriage meant commitment and celibacy, or did once. He'd never tried holding to one woman's couch for long and he doubted he had it in him. It wasn't done. Why should he? Gods shared themselves with many lovers. Admitting that wouldn't aid him. "We had an understanding in Greece and she'd accepted."

"When is the wedding?" shouted a young woman, with small features and a wide mouth, waving her hand above the field of reporters.

"Are you planning to elope?" said a balding man in front.

Dr. Priam gave him an inquisitive tilt of her head.

Apollo smiled. "We haven't decided." That wasn't a lie, not entirely. He hadn't said anything really.

Cassie's mother nodded toward a burly agent

at her flank. "It's too much. I can't go on." Dr. Priam lifted her hand to her brow and swooned into the arms of the nearby agent.

Another officer stepped forward "Dr. Priam is exhausted by the events. The interview is over. Information will be forthcoming as it's made available."

The mob disbanded with a low murmur. The agents snagged Apollo by the arms and they followed Dr. Priam into the house and to a room where the furniture was elegant, attractive and uncomfortable. So like Cassie's mother. Apollo could have rendered them all still as stone, but chose to hear them out. He sat upon a high-backed green chair after Dr. Priam took a seat across from him on the couch.

Three agents hovered beside her, a wall of muscle and weaponry between Apollo and Cassie's mother. "How do you know my daughter?"

"As I said, I met her at Delphi and things went from there."

She leaned forward. "Stop it. Cassie's never mentioned a man like you and she's certainly never spoken of an engagement. That I would've heard. What are you trying to pull? I don't even know your name." Two more agents entered the room, one positioned at Apollo's right and another at his left. The energy shifted and Apollo felt their intent to take him in.

This woman was worthy of a god's smite, but

she was also Cassie's mother. He would bear her disrespect. "I'm Apollo and I met Cassandra in Greece. I asked her to stay with me, and she ..." What could he say? "She wanted to finish her education and would think about what I'd said."

"You're not John Medina?" Cassie's mother stared at him cold-eyed. One of the agents' lips twitched. He must know the man.

Apollo seized the opportunity. "You there. Am I Medina?"

The agent flinched at being singled out. "No sir. I've met John and you're not him."

Dr. Priam considered Apollo with new interest. It reminded him of a python sizing him up before offering to squeeze the life from him. "Well, Mr. Apollo. What do you know about what's happened to Cassie?"

"She'd met Medina for dinner. I urged her against it, but you know how stubborn Cassie is."

Dr. Priam nodded slowly. "Yes. She has a mind of her own."

"I don't know what happened. She was to meet me this morning, but never arrived." What a lie he'd just told. He winced from the pain it caused his head and rubbed his brow.

"Is there anything wrong?" said Mrs. Priam, her eyes wary as a cat on the prowl.

"No, just a headache."

"I find it odd that Cassie's never mentioned you or the engagement." She narrowed her gaze to tiny blue beads. "You don't seem to be a man desperate for female companionship. I don't mean to be indelicate, but Cassie is awkward. If you think she has money, you're mistaken. What do you want with her?"

"Cassandra is not awkward." The muscles in his jaw worked. The woman was insolent. He'd like to set her at the edge of the Mediterranean and let the tide silence her, but Zeus forbade him. "Cassie is beautiful and intelligent," he growled. "She cares for people. And I love her."

The agents stared straight ahead. Cassie's mother relaxed. "That's the first true thing you've said since you walked in here." She leaned forward. "I'm glad to see that you care for her. But I am worried; Cassie went missing after 9 pm last night. It's noon. No one has seen her. I wouldn't be concerned, except this is so unlike Cassie. We had a little argument. You know how mothers and daughters are."

"Yes," he said, hiding his irritation.

"I know she had a problem," she said. "Cassie came home last night looking like, well, not herself. I have no idea where she went, but she's a naive girl for her age and was in such a state. I fear she's gotten into trouble." This time the fear in Dr. Priam's eyes was genuine.

Apollo thought that the woman might have some love for her daughter after all. "There's no place she'd go, no friend she'd call?"

"I've contacted everyone she knows and no one has seen her. I was hoping you might have answers."

"I wish I did. We'd had a fight." Apollo shrugged. "She was angry when she left."

Cassie's mother rose to her feet, indignation burning hot in her gaze. "Did you see her last night? Are you the one who tore her blouse and God knows what else?" The agents moved in closer. "I think the officers will continue this conversation. Get him out of here."

The men encircled Apollo as Dr. Priam sneered, making her look old and hard.

They were about to lay hands on him and he wouldn't permit that.

* * *

Cassie heard her mother's outraged shriek and shuffled into the room. Raising her brows in surprise at what met her gaze—her mother and Apollo scowling at each other. "What are you doing here?" Apollo looked, like always, gorgeous, but also shadowed with concern. "Have you both been looking for me? I haven't been gone twenty-four hours. Really Mom, you do have a gift for drama. Dad will just love this. I see you called in the big guns. Is it the entire FBI or just the locals?"

"You didn't come home last night. I was worried." Her mom lifted her chin.

"I'm twenty five years old, Mother. I can take care of my self." She glared at her mom, not ready to forgive her just yet.

"And you." She stared at Apollo standing amidst the agents. "What are you doing here? I don't want to talk to you."

Apollo moved toward her, but the agents blocked his path. He grumbled a few words beneath his breath.

Her mother interjected. "This young man expects me to believe that you're engaged to him. Is that true?"

Something groaned inside of Cassie, a mix of excitement, hope and annoyance. "Really. You never mentioned marriage."

"I knew it," quipped her mother.

He pulled at the collar of his white shirt. "My commitment was understood."

"Ha!" Cassie plopped herself into a straight-backed chair. "Expecting you to be committed is as likely as a cat."

Dr. Priam excused the agents with a nod. "We need to discuss this alone."

As they left, Cassie crossed her arms over her belly and shot her mother a warning gaze. She was not having this conversation in front of her mom. "Whatever Apollo and I have to say to each other doesn't involve you."

"But..."

Cassie cut her off. "Leave, Mom, or I'm calling back those reporters. They're still camped out across the street. I had to climb the neighbor's fence to get here unseen. I'm sure they'd love the story of what your daughter did last night and where she'd slept."

"Humph." Her mom stiffened at the swipe and stomped from the room.

Cassie's head pounded and her mouth felt like she'd swallowed a wad of paper towels. What happened at the bar last night was fuzzy, just like her tongue. She didn't think she'd be able to stand the sight of iced tea again without hurling. And she didn't need her mother playing diva to the media when she'd arrived home or Apollo looking like, well, something good to wake up to. The man might be the cure to her wounds, but then, he'd caused most of them, and Cassie refused to let him off easy. She'd had enough hurt from her mom, John and all the other disappointing relationships life threw at her. She didn't need Apollo adding to it.

She breathed in to thwart the ache between her ears and focused on Apollo through stinging eyes. "I'm grateful that you showed up at John's when you did, but I wouldn't have been there in the first place if it weren't for you. I'd still be with Eric. You manipulated to keep men from my life. I saw what you did to Medina. Is that how you scared off Eric and the rest? Why did you do that anyway? And don't tell me it was for my own good, because that's a lie." She waited for him to explain. *This should be good.*

He loosened the top button of his shirt, shed his navy jacket and tossed it onto the couch. With all that movement, she got a whiff of his scent, sweet nectar, and with each intake of her breath, the stabbing behind her eyes dissipated. She breathed in again, hungry for his aroma.

It wasn't fair that he affected her this way. Cassie knew from the first time she'd seen him in her dreams that he might be the man for her, but he hadn't been real. Now he was, but it was still destined to fail. She had to follow what made sense, even amid the alcoholic fuzz in her head. She took in another breath. The throbbing in her temples dissolved and Cassie felt too good to be angry. Yet she refused to let it go. "I'm waiting."

He lowered his gaze. The action reminded her of a repentant puppy, a golden retriever she'd had as a child. She'd loved that dog. Max could chew up her best shoes, but when he scampered to her, with her sneaker still in his mouth slobbery with his drool, his eyes sparking with joy, she couldn't stay mad. Apollo was the same way.

He deserved being put in his kennel for bad behavior, but she just couldn't do it.

"I understand." He stared at her with that look, the one that said I'm sorry, and I'll never do it again, and even if you scream at me, I'll still love you forever.

Damn, he was good. "Why did you do it? Why did you run off every man that walked into my life? Not that there were all that many to begin with."

With a few strides, he took his place in front of her. His gaze softened as he looked into her face.

"Some were as bad as I'd told you. One was despicable like that insect, John Medina." He placed his hands on her upper arms and stroked his fingers up and down her skin.

Tingles shot through her and made it difficult to think. She forced her thoughts away from his touch. "They couldn't all be dangerous."

"They weren't worthy of you. I wouldn't have you give yourself to an undeserving mortal."

"Who were you to decide who was deserving? I'm sure in your mind, the only man worthy of my affection is you?" Steam built in her gut, threatening to rise.

"I care for you." His fingers slid up her neck and rubbed away building tension. "I know your heart. I've always loved you, but you had closed yourself off to me."

"When did I do that?"

"After Troy. When insanity took your mind, it also took your heart."

"Right," she snorted. "You say that because I didn't fall into your bed."

"If it had been only that." He narrowed his gaze, seeming to see past her defenses. "You stubbornly refused my healing and comfort, though you sorely needed it. The damage scarred your heart and cankered your soul. You shut out more than me, Cassandra, you shut out any chance at love."

Had losing her mind in that early life put a wedge between her and relationships? Maybe. But her dating failures weren't just about her. Apollo had interfered, damaged her confidence and hurt her. The blade twisting in her stomach from each breakup remained sharp. He needed to know it. "Do you realize what your actions cost me? All the nights I cried over being dumped without the courtesy of knowing why. When all my friends had dates and boyfriends, and gushed over their latest love, I listened with a raw heart because I had nothing. You did that. You, with your selfish possession, you never thought about the price I paid."

"I thought about it." He leaned closer, his mouth a kiss away.

She reared back and shook her head to deny the desire clouding her mind. "I'm attracted to you, but attraction isn't a relationship. I need friendship and a man I can trust. Someone who can think of my needs as well as his own, and apparently you're incapable. Get out."

His eyes widened. "What? But I'm helping you." He dropped his hands from her. "You need time. I'll talk to you after you've calmed down."

"Are you incapable of listening? I don't want to talk to you. Ever. Find yourself another girl. As I recall, the past is littered with your women. Why not look up Daphne? She was supposed to be one of your great loves."

"I'll ignore that reference to my past because I can see that you're upset."

"Damn right, I'm upset." She seethed with

frustration and considered smacking him.

"I am sorry." He looked at her with his puppy dog eyes. "I...I didn't understand. I do now."

"How could you understand? You're a freaking god." She spit the accusation at him. "You've never suffered a day in your very long existence. What do you know about real pain?"

Apollo pulled her to him, caging her in his arms and lowered his head to within inches from her face. She stiffened, anger burning in her veins. His gaze darkened. "How can you believe that I've never suffered?"

His voice was low and thick with emotion. "You were tormented and I've repented for millennia for my part in it. I close my eyes and I can still see your agony. Zeus shackled me. Even now I can feel the chains cutting into my flesh. He refused my pleas to save you. Your cries and mine were denied."

"Suffering?" His jaw hardened and his grip on her dug into her soft flesh. "Imagine having the one you adore raped in front of you, beaten, kidnapped and forced to be a concubine, no, a prize of war. And then imagine you had the power to strike the slime dead, to cast your gaze and turn them all to ash." His blue eyes flashed red. "Zeus made me impotent, left to watch the horrors that took your body, then your mind and finally your life." He let her go, his eyes retuning to their azure blue. "No, my love, I know nothing of suffering."

His words shook her to her core. Tears welled in her eyes. "I didn't know. In my dreams as Cassandra, I was alone. You were never there, if you at least had come and stayed with me — after."

"I did, but you'd closed yourself off and refused to see me."

A tear slid down her cheek. Had stubbornness forced her to suffer alone? "Why can I see you now when I'm determined to shut you out?"

"Ah Cassie, You're not as determined as you'd like to think. Part of you is desperate to heal the past because you know we're meant to be together."

She stared at him, waiting for his truthful glow to fade. It didn't.

Damn.

He cupped her face in his hands and took her mouth with a soft, gentle press of lips that warmed her. She wanted more of him. Cassie reached up and buried her fingers in his mane. Their tongues danced, caressed and stroked. Each pass built a fire in her blood. This was no safe brush of lips. Kissing Apollo burned down to her soul igniting passion. She'd done this and more with him in her dreams. Her face heated. Real surpassed the fantasy.

One of his hands left her face and slid down her spine to the small of her back. He held her against him. She couldn't miss the evidence of his want. She breathed in his honeyed aroma. Everything about him made her mouth water and fed desire. Cassie leaned against him.

He broke off the kiss.

Shaken by the abrupt end, she blinked and focused on his face. His eyes swirled with need, his full lips moist and inviting.

Apollo nodded behind her in the direction of the open door. "She's watching," he whispered.

Cassie jerked her head toward the door. "Mother. I'm sure those reporters are still outside."

The sound of her mother's pumps shuffling away on the carpet eased Cassie's frustration. "Sorry." She looked at the man holding her, safe in his arms. Was Apollo the man destined to be her love? "I need to think."

"Don't think too long. There's the embassy to consider."

That wasn't what she'd meant. Cassie sighed as the weight of people's lives burdened her shoulders. "I know." Prickles danced at the back of her neck and she rubbed them away with her fingers. "I guess we're stuck with each other."

Apollo brushed her lips with his. "Stuck? I prefer joined." He kissed his way to her ear. "For eternity."

She swallowed. "First Hydra, then you. I can only handle one mythological beast at a time."

He raised his golden head and smiled. "I'm not a beast. An animal at times, but not a beast."

CHAPTER TWELVE

Apollo left Cassie's home and wondered how he'd help her now that prophecy was no longer a tool. He had no minions and Zeus frowned on divine assistance without his order. His father preferred that his children prove themselves alone. Apollo didn't enjoy thinking on the tasks others had tackled for to gain favor. Heracles and Perseus had both performed feats worthy of a god. What would Zeus require from him?

His wager with Hades pressed on his mind. It wasn't the frustration of serving his uncle, though that irritated him, but the thought of Cassie in the underworld; never again able to enjoy the beauty of this life or the pleasures he might have brought her. That was the true worry that stabbed like a javelin and crushed his heart like a millstone. To save Cassie from that fate, he'd suffer anything.

But what could he do? He must have knowledge of Hydra and needed minions to gain it. Relying on mortals chafed his hide. He hadn't visited Earth in a while, but there might still be a few women in Athens that might help—if they were still speaking to him.

Taking that path required a trip to Greece. Not that he minded, but he refused to leave Cassie alone. He'd have to convince her to accompany him and that meant a plane. On his own, he could travel by thought, but Cassie required other modes of transportation. Apollo didn't relish climbing into a metal tube and trusting human science to get them off the ground. That required more faith in mortal ingenuity than he possessed, but for Cassie, he'd endure even that flimsy construct.

It made him think of those small cans with sardines crammed close together until there wasn't space enough to slip in a blade. He sighed. This would be more of a struggle than he'd thought. Maybe Cassie was right and he didn't know true suffering, but he had the feeling he'd soon find out.

* * *

Cassie laid on her bed, thinking over her conversation with Apollo. She'd never considered that he'd suffered. His passionate explanation made his pain real to her. He did care. She'd always wondered about the gods. How it would be to wield powers and superhuman strength? She understood there were pitfalls. Nothing was perfect, whether one was a mortal or a god, but this revelation of Apollo castrated from his power gave her a new understanding of hell.

Maybe Zeus didn't struggle and everything worked the way he wanted. He made the laws, after all, but Apollo battled as much as she did. Zeus was a tyrant demanding to be obeyed, and it made her dad look like a teddy bear. The gods were cruel.

But Apollo didn't have a mother like hers. His mother had died anciently, so he didn't have her pushing his buttons and making him crazy. Cassie had that over him. "Lucky me," she said to the air. But she did have a mother—selfish at times, but deep down Cassie knew her mom loved her. She meant well, she just lacked tact.

Cassie called her dad again. What was it with him? He usually kept his word and called if he said he would. "Ugh."

She stood and stripped off the torn blouse, jeans and underwear. She would enjoy a hot shower, and then read up on the embassy, list what she recalled from her dreams, and then make a plan. She'd have to rely on Apollo and his prophetic gift to figure out what to do next.

After the shower relaxed her shoulders and helped clear her mind, Cassie turned on the television in her room to catch up on the news of the day. She braided her hair and then pulled out clean jeans and a blue sweatshirt from her drawer. Cassie slipped them on during the commercial. She loved the feel of the cotton against her skin, so comfortable and relaxed. Why her mother favored rigid, form-fitting clothes amazed her, but then, that's who her mother was, rigid and fitted.

The television screen filled with the sight of her dad entering the U S embassy in Athens. Cassie stared at the television and cranked up the volume with the remote.

The announcer's voice blared:

"The US secretary of state is meeting with world leaders to discuss the situation. Hydra has claimed responsibility for the bombing of Rome's train station. The group has made no demands, but meetings are scheduled to discuss a plan of action. Hydra is an international organization possibly centered in Turkey with ties around the globe. Hydra believes lasting change can only be achieved through violence, destroying the status quo and creating something new. Many governments disagree and hope to negotiate peace with Hydra.

The Pope has called for a day of prayer and an end to violence. As I stand before the smoldering remnants in Rome, I can only hope that some of the victims of this tragedy are found alive and an agreement can be made with this new terrorist threat."

Cassie sucked in a breath. Her hands, already moist with perspiration, she switched the channel to another station.

"Secretary Priam will be meeting in the U S embassy in Athens. Hydra was once believed to be a small group of activists, consisting mostly of students and disgruntled youth that couldn't find work in the current economy, and no real danger. That belief was proven false late last night after a series of bombs exploded along the train lines between Rome and Naples. The damage to the system is extensive. Naples port is closed and ships await instructions on where to unload their cargo. The real tragedy is the rising death toll. It will take days, perhaps weeks, to uncover the bodies trapped below the surface and access the damage. There's one thing for certain, the world is awake to a new enemy."

She turned off the television and lowered herself to the edge of the bed on wobbly legs. Her heart raced and stuck in her throat making it hard to swallow. It had happened. Hydra was active and killing innocent people. Her gut twisted as the dream of destruction rattled her mind. Hydra must be stopped. She had to find a way. And now her dad was in Athens, the target of the next disaster.

Cassie had to get to Greece and do what ever it took to make her dad believe her. She'd chain herself to the doors of the embassy if need be and scream until someone listened. Her dad in danger. The prickle at the back of her neck warned and she feared.

She made arrangements for the next flight to Greece. To hell with the danger. If she could convince Apollo to join her, she'd be safer than anyone on the planet. He was a god. An entire army might want to take down the plane and it wouldn't happen. Apollo wouldn't let it. "Oh, but wait. That hadn't saved Troy," she murmured. The knots in her stomach floated in a sea of acid. "And John had almost." A shiver crawled down her spine. "Well, Apollo did get there in time."

Last night, Cassie woke up lying on a cot in the storage room in the back of the bar. She'd found that drinking heavily didn't improve anything and wasn't her cup of tea. Her stomach rolled at the thought of any kind of tea. The vision of the tawny beverage spraying over the asphalt didn't help.

Never doing that again.

"What am I doing? I have to pack." She jumped to her feet, dragged out her suitcase and threw clothes into it. Just a few things.

She wouldn't be gone long, but while she was, she'd find out more from Apollo about his conversation with her mother. Did he really tell her they were engaged? Why invent that lie? The word "engaged" linked to marriage and she couldn't believe Apollo wanted anything so serious. Did he?

She tried to divert her mind, but her mother's mocking tone continued to eat at Cassie. Why couldn't she be engaged? Was it that impossible to consider? Sure, she'd been dumped by every man she'd dated, but that hadn't been her fault. Not entirely, she hoped.

Apollo might be sincere and love her. "Yeah, right," she muttered. "And I might be a goddess with hoards of men worshipping at my feet." Cassie tossed a deck of cards into her purse for the long flight and finished packing. "He's a god. Not happening." But her thoughts remained on Apollo. Frustrated at herself for considering—no, wanting—the engagement to be true. Silly. Was she so desperate that she entertained fairytales? Damn, was she really that hung up on the guy?

"Enough already." She turned her mind to her dad. Apollo had to know that he was in Athens just as he'd known that she was about to show up at her house. He'd wanted to catch her stumbling through the door with a head that felt the size of Texas throbbing on her shoulders. Of course, he knew everything. Apollo probably had the whole thing planned and would meet her in Greece.

Cassie hauled her suitcase off the bed, snatched her purse and raced downstairs. Adrenaline ran through her veins, bubbling up and churning her stomach. When she reached the bottom of the stairs and the entry, there stood Apollo. He didn't wear his usual toga or a suit, but dressed in military camo. And he looked uneasy.

* * *

Apollo stared at her. She looked beautiful with her hair tied back in a braid, her cheeks flushed with color, and her violet eyes bright with excitement. He wished he'd caused that look. She carried a suitcase as if she intended to leave on a trip. She had no prophetic gift, not any longer, and he hadn't told her his plans. Like him, Cassie must have gleaned the situation from mortal news.

"I have us on the next military flight to Greece," he said, watching for her reaction.

"Oh, I'll cancel my domestic flight. How did you manage that?"

"I have contacts. We're accompanying General Hector. We need to hurry if we're going to get there in time." Not a complete lie, but he'd used divine abilities to ensure their flight. He didn't look forward to sitting in the belly of the aircraft among so many soldiers. He knew these winged monstrosities usually flew without mishap. Usually.

She blinked at him and put her bag down by her feet. "General Hector? Five star General Hector?"

"The same. Why?"

"Dad said that he was in his office just the other day. How did you arrange this?"

"I have my ways." Of course, a little god-like persuasion helped.

"Let's go." Cassie hefted her suitcase, but Apollo took it from her.

"Allow me." He wouldn't have her carrying for herself when he could without any effort.

"Thanks." She smiled. Her lips curved in a perfect temptation and he took the opportunity to kiss her.

She didn't argue, but slid her arms around his neck and leaned in.

He dropped the bag, rested his hands over her round hindquarters and delved into her mouth with his tongue. She moaned. The aroma of her hair like almonds infused with woman spurred him on. He wanted to indulge himself with more of her, and caress her soft skin hidden beneath her jeans, and taste from her lips, down to her navel and beyond. He squeezed the softness beneath his hands.

She pulled back. "I um, guess we should be going."

They arrived moments before take-off. General Hector shook Cassie's hand and smiled, though the shadows in his dark eyes told her something else occupied his mind. "Glad to have you aboard."

"Thanks for including us," she said.

"Including you?" The general wrinkled his brow as if confused. His military cut displayed the full concern on his weathered face. "Just following orders."

She glanced to Apollo. He shrugged. "Orders." He couldn't explain surrounded by people, but she seemed to accept well enough.

Cassie and Apollo sat together near the front of the plane. She slipped on her safety belt and he almost laughed at how ridiculous it was. As if that little strip of fabric could keep her from falling out of the heavens. Mortals were beyond gullible. The rest of the people on board did the same.

She stared at him and nodded to the scrap of

cloth in his lap. "Well?" she said. "Aren't you going to buckle up?"

He still thought the exercise was pointless, but he clipped the buckle ends together around his hips and did his best to appear satisfied that this made all the difference in his safety. He would have laughed had he not been concerned about the metal tube's ability to lift from the ground, loaded with the weight of men and women and a few thousand pounds of equipment.

The engines roared and Apollo clutched the arms of his seat. He forced himself to talk with Cassie to distract from the creaking plane as it rumbled over the tarmac.

Her mouth twitched before a wide grin took over her features. "It's your first time flying, isn't it?"

He grinned with false confidence. "No. I've flown many times, just not using a metal box with wings pasted on." Sweat trickled down his back and under his arms. He hadn't felt this nervous awaiting his father's decree of punishment.

Cassie reached over and covered his hand with hers. "It's not bad. After we're in the air, it's smooth. You'll forget that we're flying ten thousand feet above Earth."

"This isn't helping," he said.

She snickered. "Sorry, but it really is the safest form of transportation there is."

"Not for me." His hands were moist and cool. He tightened his grip on the arms of his seat as the contraption picked up speed. The metal tube shook. Apollo trembled along with the plane. They lifted into the air and the shaking ended. The quiver and squeak ceased. The only sound was the hum of the engines. Apollo's fingers ached from tension. The knots in his shoulders relaxed and he exhaled with relief.

"See it's fine," said Cassie, patting his hand. "You'll learn to like it. You can read or take a nap, and you don't have to think about anything."

"Not quite. We have plenty to think about."

Her violet gaze turned purple and her smile faded. "I'll do my best to convince my dad. Now that he's seen the destruction firsthand, maybe he'll believe me."

A confused look must have covered his face, "Your father? But he's not in Greece."

She stared at him and blinked. "He's there now. A series of bombs hit Rome, destroyed the train station, and killed hundreds of people." Her lips parted. "You didn't know. How is it that you didn't know about this?" Her olive skin paled to a lighter tint and the vibrant rose of her mouth along with it.

"I..." What could he say? The truth would be best. "Zeus has taken my gift of prophecy in punishment for manipulating your life, among other offenses. We must act without it."

She sat back with her head against the seat and her eyes trained on the ceiling. "Great. As if this wasn't going to be difficult enough, now we can't stay one step ahead of the enemy. Hydra is very bad news." She leaned toward him and focused on his face. "Didn't you hear about any of this? Ugh, of course you wouldn't. Well, they're monsters as dangerous as the mythological creature. And they mean to destroy what ever they can. They haven't given a reason for their actions and no demands have been made." She twisted the end of her seat belt with her fingers. "How in this world are we supposed to stop them now?"

Cassie was obviously upset with the current situation. In truth, so was he, but he wouldn't admit it. "We will succeed. I know Athens and the embassy intimately. We will stop them."

She scowled and yanked on the end of her braid. "How can you be so sure? We don't even know what they want."

Apollo did know. Hydra wanted what every despotic, dictatorial faction had wanted since the beginning of time. He leveled his gaze on Cassie and hated sharing what he knew to be fact. "They desire one thing. Power. And they will pay any price to get it."

"Any price?" Cassie's mouth trembled. "So there will be no negotiating with them. You're sure about this?"

"I'm positive. There may be a show of working something out, but it's only to purchase time until they put their plans into action. Hydra wants to make a statement. Striking fear into the hearts of men is only the beginning."

* * *

Cassie closed her eyes as the plane rumbled on to Greece. Talking to her dad had to work. Maybe Apollo could convince him. He must have done a miraculous job of it to get them on this military flight—faster than domestic and no stops.

They hit rough air and the plane bounded up and down, jerked and fell until her stomach rested in her throat before leveling off again. Apollo had a stranglehold on the armrests. With his strength, he might crush them or rip them free from the seat. That would be tough to explain. Perspiration dotted his upper lip. She'd never thought that a god might be afraid of anything. He looked on the edge of being sick. She dug in the seat back in front of her and handed him a barf bag. "Here. Just in case."

Apollo pried one hand loose and took the sack. He snarled as he read the instructions printed on the outside. "I have no need of this." He gave it back to her.

She hoped he was right. Maybe all he needed was distraction. "Do you want to play cards?"

He turned his head in a stiff but quick motion. His skin held an unhealthy pallor—not quite green, but on the way there. "Are you sure you're okay? You'll feel better if you can take your mind off the flight."

Apollo peeled his finger from the armrests.

"What game do you suggest?"

"Poker might be good, but the stakes have to be high enough to keep you engaged. What should we play for?"

His mouth twisted and then formed a weak smile. "Not coin. I have no need for it."

"I thought as much. How about playing for something that's important to you. Is there anything like that, something you'd hate to lose?"

He stared down at her and gave a slight nod. "Yes, I can wager my lyre."

Her eyes widened. "Really? The lyre you gained from Hermes? Wow. I'll take that bet." She thought about what she owned for exchange. Whatever she had couldn't be of value to a god. There was one thing. "Okay, I put on the table a night together. If I win, I get your lyre. If you win, you get a night with me."

His eyes brightened. "Agreed."

She'd toyed with the fantasy of sleeping with him ever since Delphi. His invasion into her dreams had made her comfortable with the idea and now the thought brought longing and warmth low in her belly. Having sex with a god was the stuff of legend, but it was Apollo's explanation of how he'd suffered for her that clinched it. If she were to have sex only once in her life, which seemed likely considering their situation, then she wanted it to be memorable.

Cassie pulled her purse onto her lap and rummaged for her deck of cards. "What do you want to play, straight-up poker or something wild?"

He licked his lips. "If I'm playing for a night with you, beloved, something wild, absolutely."

Her cheeks must have turned bright red gauging from their sudden heat and Apollo's grin. Would he notice if she cheated to lose? Because no matter what else happened, she refused to die before knowing the joys of making love with Apollo.

They played a hand. She won the first, he the next, and before the third, she yawned. Exhaustion bore into her eyes. "How about we take a break? I need to catch some sleep before we arrive or I won't be worth anything when we get there."

"I think you're afraid you'll lose and are avoiding it." His mouth turned up at the edges, and he looked in much better spirits than when they'd left.

"I'm not running out on you. I finish what I start." She yawned and her jaw popped. "Ouch. Seriously, I'll be brain dead if I don't get some sleep." Cassie leaned back against her seat and closed her eyes. "You could play a tune on that harp of yours."

"It's not a harp, it's a lyre," he grumbled.

She knew the difference between a harp and a lyre. She'd messed with him in an effort to distract from his fear of flying. "You could play something restful for the troops." She stole a look from a slit eye. He already had the lyre in his hands and tuned it. Cassie chuckled to herself. That should keep him busy for hours.

* * *

Apollo played to the backdrop of snores, the rumble of engines and the occasional soft sigh from Cassie as she slept. The woman captivated him. She toyed with him. He'd missed her humor and playfulness. It's what had originally drawn him to her when she served at Delphi.

The gods believed it was Cassandra's virtue or her beauty that enticed him. While those reasons were compelling, they didn't call his heart to entwine about hers. Their souls had united through millennia, like trees planted beside one another, and grown together over time into one trunk. The roots entangled so that to remove one meant the death of the other. This was how it was meant to be between men and women. Separate yet one, acting as each other's shade, protection and strength.

Cassie was all of that to him, and this incarnation of the woman with her wit, compassion and humor had bound his heart to hers. And he wanted this tethering to her soul. She'd done all she could to understand her gift, but she'd also grown to understand herself. Her courage surfaced. Cassie had fought the rodent and argued with Apollo. She gave no thought to her own safety, but raced to aid her father and stop Athens' destruction.

He'd loved this woman for ages. His heart ached for her and because of her. He adored her above all others. And he'd tasted enough fruit to speak with certainty. After three thousand years of waiting for his Cassandra, he refused to let her go. He couldn't lose her again.

If mighty Zeus could decree and all creation bowed, then Apollo, as a son of Zeus could also decree in this one thing: No matter what, his soul would remain with Cassie through eternity.

She had slept for hours. He could've woken her, but couldn't resist gazing on her beauty as she slept, knowing that she needed rest. He'd ceased serenading the group hours ago and rested himself. He considered the strategy he'd employ. It would be easy enough to gain access to her father, but thwarting Hydra would require effort. Hydra. The name gnawed at him. He'd heard something about the creature recently before they'd attacked the train. What had he heard or had he seen something? The answer ran from him on swift feet. He couldn't waste time on it. He needed a plan.

He glanced at the deck of cards resting in Cassie's lap. He'd let her win the next hand. When she gave herself to him. It wouldn't be over a lost wager. Love would place her in his bed.

CHAPTER THIRTEEN

Apollo had changed out of the camo and into a linen jacket and slacks to be less conspicuous. He and Cassie waited on a bench outside her father's hotel in Athens. Cassie fidgeted with her braid, her irritation palpable in the humid Mediterranean air. "What a frustrating call. If only my dad would listen to me, but no. I'm just his 'princess.' I'll need proof. Are you sure you can't tell my dad who you are? It shouldn't take much to convince him after the attack on Rome. Leave someone hanging from the ceiling or burn something with your vision. That was a nice trick when you singed off John's hair. How about doing any of that?"

He sighed. "I dare not."

"You did it before." She folded her arms over her chest. "I stretched the truth and told my dad I had great news and had to see him. Okay, it was a lie, but I had to gain face time. I thought you could convince him." She glanced over her shoulder and then focused on Apollo.

"Zeus punished me for just such acts. He was

lenient last time and warned me against defying him again." Apollo cringed to think how Zeus might afflict him.

"What does that even mean?" Cassie scanned to her left, shrugged and then jumped to her feet. "I can't sit here anymore. I know Zeus is a cruel SOB., but you're his son. He wouldn't do anything to hurt you, not like the myth of Prometheus. Zeus would never chain you to a mountain and let birds peck at your liver. Would he?"

Apollo's stomach twisted from the truth of his father's violence. How could he make her understand that the gods were ruthless? They might be difficult to kill, but it was possible. And because they possessed a long life, they valued living not more, but less. Replacing Apollo would be as easy for Zeus as lying with another beautiful woman. And someone always caught his father's roving eye. "The gods exist under a different set of laws from men. Zeus rules. No matter our connection or how much we may disagree with him, we're commanded to follow or suffer the consequences." He let out a frustrated breath. "Zeus is guilty of more savagery than you can comprehend."

"Those horrible stories are true?" Cassie's face paled and she regained her seat. "Even the tale of Medusa with her head covered in snakes?"

"The story varies some, but yes, the Gorgon was cursed with unsightly serpents. It's just one example of punishments decreed on gods and men."

"Men?" Her eyes widened. "But the gods don't involve themselves on earth anymore."

"Not that you'd be able to tell."

"Then they do intervene on occasion?" A twinkle lit Cassie's eyes and Apollo didn't like the look of it.

"If Zeus commands it."

"Then you could visit your father and ask him to intervene with Hydra. It's possible he'd agree and keep this horror from happening," Cassie pleaded.

Apollo's shoulders tensed. "You don't know what you're asking. Zeus hasn't forgotten my last offense. If I ask so soon, he might make things worse." Something was wrong with the situation beyond the obvious threat. His gut gnawed at him. "An immortal is involved. I'm sure of it. It might be that half brother of mine, Hermes. He's been a trickster since birth and I've never trusted Hades." Apollo's inner fire smoldered at the mention of his uncle.

Cassie's gaze narrowed. "You're punished for a little light show while the other gods get away with murder. That's just sick and wrong. You have to go to Zeus and stop them from interfering. If they are working against us, they should be punished."

"They will be if Zeus sees fit to act. I'm in no position to demand anything and Zeus doesn't always see things the way we do. Nothing gets past my father, believe me. He knows everything."

She jumped up and stomped her foot. The soft sole made little sound, muffling the effect. "That's just great. And there's nothing to be done about it?"

"About Zeus? No."

"Ugh!" She threw her hands into the air. "There must be something?"

He understood her frustration, but raging wouldn't help. "We're on our own." Apollo feared using godly persuasion on her father. He'd bent mortal will gaining the flight to Greece and dared not do it again. Zeus had warned him.

Cassie glanced to her right.

"What are you doing? You look like a creature being stalked."

She rubbed at the base of her skull. "I feel someone watching me."

He shook his head. "Not someone, men. Haven't you noticed how you look in those jeans?"

Cassie's cell phone pinged and she pulled it from her purse. "Dad's ready to meet us."

She showed her identification when the agents stopped her in the hotel. Two burly men narrowed their eyes on Apollo. "Your ID, and we'll need to check you for weapons."

"No," said Apollo glaring at them. The indignity brought him close to leaving the men prostrate. He chose a simpler course and walked right by them.

The agents returned her ID. "This way." They escorted her down the hall. Cassie glanced at Apollo as they walked together, confusion furrowing her brow. "What happened?" she whispered.

One stocky older agent glanced at her. "You'll need to ask the secretary."

Apollo smiled. "They can't see or hear me."

The younger agent knocked on a door and it opened.

"Nice trick," said Cassie.

The agent glanced at her and shrugged.

Secretary Priam smiled when he saw Cassie and hugged her. The aging diplomat's demeanor changed when he noticed Apollo, his mouth puckered as if tasting bad wine. "And this is?"

Cassie forced a too-tight grin. "Dad, this is my, um...friend, Apollo. We have something important to discuss with you and the sooner the better."

"What's all of this about? I can think of only one reason my daughter would fly halfway around the world with a young man and tell me it's urgent. Are you thinking of getting married?" Secretary Priam stared hard at Apollo. "What is your name, what do you do, and why should I let you marry my daughter?"

Apollo clamped down on his annoyance as Mr. Priam sized him up like a horse he considered buying and doubted his worth. *This is for Cassie.*

Her face flushed red as hibiscus petals. "Dad,

That's not it at all. We have information."

She nodded toward Apollo. He believed in the truth and they might as well begin there. "Hydra plans to attack the US embassy here in Athens."

Her father stepped closer to Apollo, his eyes leveled in challenge. "Hydra has publicly threatened Rome, not Greece. We're meeting with them to negotiate a deal. You have it wrong."

"That's only to put you off," said Apollo, mustering his patience. This mortal all but called him a liar. A low growl rumbled in his throat. He didn't suffer this treatment from anyone but Zeus. How long could he bear it?

"You sound very sure of yourself. How did you come by this information?"

Tension crept up Apollo's neck like spidery legs. He had to say something, but the truth would gain him severe displeasure from Zeus. Could he tempt fate, alter the man's thinking, and force his agreement to act? A temptation, but better to follow his father's command. "I have a source. It's highly reliable."

"*You* have a source." The secretary smirked.

The last mortal that dared look at Apollo that way, ceased to exist. Patience.

Her father shifted his gaze to Cassie. "Why did you bring him here if he won't talk? I don't have time for this."

"But Dad, it's the truth. You have to believe us." Her eyes glistened with emotion. "People will die if you don't do something."

"People *have* died," ground out her father. His jowls quivered as he shook his head. "I'm sorry, princess. I appreciate your passion, but I've met many passionate people, and if you don't have more than an anonymous tip, I can't act on it. I need facts." He herded them toward the door of his suite and hugged Cassie in a one-armed embrace. "When this is over and we're home under more pleasant circumstances, we'll talk. For now, I have work to do."

Apollo and Cassie found themselves back in the long hall with the door shut behind them. Cassie stared at Apollo. Her chin quivered and her eyes shimmered with tears. He'd seen that same look three thousand years ago when Cassandra failed to convince the king of Troy just before they wheeled that monstrous horse into the city.

* * *

Cassie's eyes burned and she blinked back tears. She would not cry. The embassy's only hope and people's lives rested on her, and she was about to fail. That messed with her more than her father brushing her aside and grilling Apollo as if he were a foolish kid. Tears blurred her vision. "I can't convince anyone."

Before she could wipe her eyes with her hand, Apollo pulled a cloth from his pocket and dabbed at her face. "Blow," he said, holding the cloth up to her nose. Cassie sucked in a breath and blew. He wiped and dabbed at her nose, and then pulled her into his arms and stroked her hair.

From what she recalled, this situation was too similar to Troy. Though Apollo hadn't taken away her gift of prophecy, Zeus had. If history was destined to repeat itself, then she was in the middle of one hell of a reenactment. She sniffed against his crisp linen jacket. "I'm sorry. It's all been for nothing." She tilted her face up and looked at him through weepy eyes. "What can we do?"

He whispered in a low voice. "Don't worry. I'll handle this."

"How?" she croaked.

"I don't know just yet, but if a god can't outwit a few mortals, then there's no hope for the universe."

He smiled and she had to believe that he told the truth. Cassie blinked away moisture. Had Apollo's glow dimmed a bit? No, that couldn't be. Her puffy eyes just distorted her view.

* * *

If Cassie's father required proof, then so be it. The man reminded Apollo of Zeus— unyielding and demanding, with little patience for anything other than his own agenda. He'd disregarded both Apollo and the attack in Athens. Arrogant, shortsighted mortal. They had to convince him or find another way.

Apollo blinked. His twin sister hovered behind Cassie. Artemis had pulled her amber-colored hair back, securing it with gold clips. Her short green dress was her usual attire for a hunt, but she lacked her bow and golden arrows. "I must speak with you," she said. "Alone."

Cassie heard nothing. Her dark head rested on his chest. "What will we do now?" she murmured.

What indeed.

Artemis stared down her long straight nose at him. "I'm waiting."

Apollo knew his sister well. She adored him and would help his cause, but while she possessed great wisdom, patience eluded her. He nuzzled the top of Cassie's head. "Beloved, I must attend to something and it may take time. Will you be alright on your own?"

She stepped back from him. "I'm not a baby. I'll be fine." She rolled her eyes. "I'll visit the market, grab some lunch since we didn't eat, and meet you at our hotel. Maybe I'll be inspired and think up a way to salvage this mess."

He didn't like leaving her, but his sister's insistence pushed him. "Excellent idea. I'll see you soon."

Cassie swung her purse over her shoulder and left.

Artemis' light blue gaze shadowed with worry. "What's this I hear of you wagering with Hades? I thought you had more sense."

He usually did, but it evaporated where Cassie was concerned. "Did you come here to reprimand me or help?"

"Both, you dolt."

"And the help?"

Her clear brow wrinkled. "I've watched our uncle. He's up to something. Hades and Zeus spend hours over that chessboard arguing. You won't believe the pieces Hades is resurrecting for the game—the Cyclops, Hydra and his terrible three-headed dog. He'll unleash the titans if he can."

Apollo flinched at the mention of them. "The titans?" They were the greatest threat to the gods, including Zeus. "Our father would never agree. The titans would destroy humanity and then come after us."

"Don't be so sure. You know how Zeus can get when he gambles."

Apollo did know. Mortal disease came by way of a lost wager. "What's at stake?"

"They won't say."

"No, they wouldn't." Apollo wished he had his gift for the future. He'd know how all of this turned out. Had Hades put into his father's mind this particular punishment? Apollo grumbled, "I'd like to burn a hole right through my uncle's withered head."

"And I'd like to see it, but be careful." She leaned close and whispered into his ear. "I'll do what I can to snare Hades, but he's as difficult to catch as water through a sieve."

"I'm grateful for the offer, but I don't want you reaping our father's wrath. He's been in a foul mood."

"Best you heed your own advice." Artemis shimmered into a green ball of light and was gone.

Apollo would be cautious. He knew many mortals in Athens. Some had been instrumental to him in the past against trouble. He'd seek them out first. Perhaps one of them knew of Hydra.

He headed for the oldest section of Athens. Striding through narrow winding streets of the Plaka, he passed small shops, cafés and white-faced houses in search of the home of a particular family and a woman from his past. Andromeda Catsoulas, a truly beautiful girl with a lovely smile. Not as attractive as Cassie, but still a pleasure.

He climbed the worn steps. The same last name etched on a metal plate near the door gave him hope. He knocked and waited. A soft voice spoke and then he heard the shuffling of feet on tile. Apollo had worn his linen jacket and his best smile to dazzle women and gain favor. The door creaked open. There stood an elderly woman with an apron tied around her thin form and her gray hair knotted atop her head in a bun. Lines creased her face giving her the look of old parchment.

"You," she gasped. Worn teeth formed her broken grin, but the familiar warmth in her brown eyes remained.

"Andromeda Catsoulas?" Apollo ventured.

"Apollo? It can't be." She rubbed her crinkled eyes. "You remind me of a man I knew over fifty years ago, but no," her frail voice trailed off. "You're the image of him. You must be his son, no grandson. My, how the years have flown."

"Yes. My name is also Apollo." This was the aged version of the young girl he'd enjoyed. His heart sank at her loss of youth and beauty. How many years had passed since they'd strolled over these streets together and shared a kiss? "I'm related to him. He told me to visit this house if I ever found myself in Athens."

"How very kind of you. Come in. Come in." She pulled the door wide open. "And how is your grandfather? He was something in his youth," she chuckled. "But back then, so was I."

He took her hand, drew it to his lips, and kissed her knuckles for memory's sake. The scent of rosemary filled his nose. "I'm sure that you're as beautiful now as the day he met you."

She shook her head. "Now that was a lie, but I forgive you for it. It was such a nice lie to hear."

He'd ask about her family. Years ago, they'd been involved in the resistance. Perhaps they were still interested in such things and might have heard something. "My...grandfather wants to hear if you married? And your brothers, what became of them?"

"No I never had the pleasure or curse of marriage." She laughed, a sound of bubbling up from her belly. "And my brothers left for America when they were still young enough to make the trip. They've done well for themselves. All I have is a young boy who runs errands for me and does a few things around the house. He should be here soon. Where is that boy?" Her old eyes shifted from here to there as she searched.

Though Apollo's efforts for information had proven fruitless, he still valued his time with her. The family had bravely hidden people fleeing the county and had smuggled weapons to the resistance during the dark days of the war. Apollo had helped them where he could. Andromeda's father had been killed and his death strengthened their resolve to fight. Time couldn't dim Apollo's respect for them. "I hope all will be well with you Andromeda, and long life."

She waved her hand in dismissal. "Your grandfather use to wish me that. I'm old enough. Bring me some other blessing from him. What did you say he was up to?"

"He's doing the same as he always has."

She nodded. "Still working the family business then?"

He smiled. "Yes."

Apollo spent another hour with her, thanked her and left. The longing for past friendships and mortal connection surprised him. He'd been gone from Earth too long. If he could manage it, he'd visit Andromeda again.

Fifty years. He doubted any of his acquaintances remained. Time cursed mankind, stealing strength and beauty. How did they suffer the ravages of aging? What if he were forced into mortality? He shook himself from the thought of relentless decline. Mortality was a curse. He doubted that he could laugh through it as Andromeda did.

Apollo made his way back to their hotel and Cassie. Together, they'd make a plan.

* * *

Cassie perused the market's offerings: salty Greek olives, fresh fruits in an array of colors, crusty loaves of bread, sausages and cheese. Everything tempted her palate.

"Bella Cassie," cried a familiar voice. She turned to see a slender man with sleek, dark hair, a prominent nose and strong chin hurry to her side. He kissed her cheek. "I thought you'd gone home to your papa. What are you doing here?"

"George? I left, but I've returned for a short visit. I miss Greece so very much." She'd enjoyed dinner with him a number of times on her visit and felt comfortable with him. Finding George was a coup. He knew everyone and might have heard something about Hydra.

"Is that all you miss?" He winked. "I'd hoped that you saved a corner in your heart for me?"

Cassie smiled into his pleasant face. George wasn't obviously handsome, but his gregarious personality made him appear more attractive the longer she'd known him. Her friends thought he was gorgeous. "Just the man I need. You hear everything and I need information."

"You think too highly of me, but I will help if I can."

She glanced side to side before she spoke in a low voice. "Have you heard anything about this group Hydra?"

His smile faded and the glint in his gaze shifted to a darker tone of brown. "We don't speak of them. They're a curse. A bunch of kids believing the way to prosperity and happiness is to take it from someone else. They'll find out soon enough that once the goose is dead, the golden eggs stop coming."

"So, you've heard of them?"

"Yes, yes. It's no secret." He raised his hand and waved it about to discount the subject. "The young men run after their leader as if he were a great one. He's just a man with anger for brains and a gift with words."

"Have you seen him? Do you know who he is and what he has planned?" She leaned forward, awaiting his reply.

He eyed her. "You are interested in these things? I'd rather fish than be bothered with political whisperings. It will all blow over with the next election. That's how it goes here."

"But do you know who the leader of Hydra is?"

"Me?" He placed his hand on his chest and his eyes widened. "No, just rumors. Why would I know such things? I might have heard something from a man at the museum, but I don't listen."

Her neck prickled like crazy, giving her the idea that he knew more than he was telling. She had to pick George's brain for a while "I want to hear about everything since I've been away. Let's share a bottle of ouzo and catch up." Cassie picked up a bottle on the way.

The two enjoyed a couple of hours, sipping the pale liquid, and renewed their friendship on the patio of his home. An afternoon breeze wafted over them and mingled the scent of lavender with the alcoholic warmth rising from her glass. She loved the city and its people. "George, I've heard that Hydra poses a danger to Athens. I'm sorry to drag you back to the subject, but if you've heard anything, or know of people that may be involved with this group, I need to know."

"I didn't realize that you believed their rhetoric." He looked up as if thinking and then returned his brown gaze to her. "Of course, if I hear anything I'll tell you. Where are you staying?"

Cassie pulled her hotel's card from her purse. "It's not far. Here's the address. I'll only be there for a few days." She stood to leave. "I hope I hear from you soon. Thank you for the lovely afternoon."

The back of her neck itched, but she couldn't tell why. George was a world traveler from she didn't know where. He'd landed in Athens years ago and had stayed. The man had little interest in politics. That's what they'd had in common—until

Apollo shifted her interest.

As she trudged past houses and shops on the way to the hotel, concern over the warning signal at the back of her neck persisted. It couldn't have anything to do with George, unless while poking around for her, he put himself in danger. No. He was warm and friendly, but also smart. He wouldn't take unnecessary chances. Prickles at the base of her skull crept down her spine. She shuddered. "Ugh. Why can't I decipher this?"

The refurbished five-story hotel sat near the market in old Athens and below the Acropolis. A fountain trickled in the courtyard: the sound of water over marble played over her ears like soothing rain. History oozed from the stone beneath her feet and she loved the local flavor.

Her mom wouldn't be caught dead there. Dr. Priam insisted on more Americanized digs. What was so great about having your own bathroom, anyway? You had to give up authentic Greece to get it. Cassie would never understand.

She entered the lobby. The clerk smiled and Cassie retuned the woman's greeting on her way to her room. Three flights of stairs and down a hall to the end. Swiping her key in the lock, she turned the knob and opened the door. Her eyes widened. Apollo was bare-butt naked. Cassie's mouth dropped open. Damn. He was beautiful.

CHAPTER FOURTEEN

Cassie should have closed the door and run.

She stood frozen by his masculine beauty. At first glance she wouldn't have believed he was real. Apollo clad in his toga was an impressive enough sight, but nude he tempted her. She continued to stare, though heat radiated from her face. It wasn't the first time she'd seen the male apparatus, but never on a naked man, and never with lust pushing her to touch.

He made no move to cover himself. Why would he? Apollo possessed the arrogant confidence of a god. And he deserved to be deified. No sculpture she'd ever seen came close to his exquisite form. The difference between the dream of Apollo and his tangible reality startled her.

Cassie licked her lips and Apollo's blue gaze flickered with heat. Primal need smoldered in those azure depths and spread to her belly. This would be her cue to leave. She cleared her throat, "Excuse me," she squeaked. "I thought this was my room."

Apollo shrugged a crisp white shirt over his broad shoulders. "It's our room." The corners of his delicious mouth curved up. "You didn't think I'd let you stay alone, did you?"

Cassie forced her gaze to his face, though with each of his movements, his open shirt revealed firm muscles leading to glimpses of his package just below the edge of his open shirt. Her breath stilled in her lungs. She learned something about herself at that moment. She wasn't afraid. Nervous standing in a room with a half-naked man, but far more comfortable than she'd ever imagined.

"Damn," she murmured. He really might be the right man for her, the one she'd dreamed of and waited for. If that were true, the relationship would work out—somehow. Cassie closed the door and leaned back against it.

"Don't be afraid. I won't touch you." A small smile teased his lips. "Unless that's what you wish."

"I'm not afraid. I just haven't..." she mumbled. Her cheeks blazed hot. The human body was a work of art. Only a child was embarrassed by a little skin.

She was not a child.

And that was the problem.

"Of course," he said. "You have limited experience with men."

Her glance fell. Limited was kind. Next to none was more accurate. She swallowed and dragged her gaze up his body landing on his tempting mouth. That trail up his chiseled abs did nothing to cool the warmth spreading in her core. Cassie's feet carried her forward to stop directly before him. How had she ever become so brazen? The feelings pulsing through her went far beyond attraction. Cassie reached out with trembling fingers and touched his chest. "Apollo."

His eyes sparked with light. He put his hand on hers and dragged it inch by inch over soft skin down his body, stopping low on his abdomen. "Are you sure?"

She quaked with anticipation. Was she sure? What woman had ever been sure of the man she was about to make love with? Her gaze fixed on his. She saw desire mingled with tenderness, and it called to her.

Focusing on his chin, she could avoid what intrigued her. "I'm not sure of anything, least of all what I want at this moment."

"You know what you want, Cassie." His voice sounded rough. "Or you wouldn't be here."

Cassie had to think this through; she'd waited so long for this experience. But sex with a god? She lifted her gaze to his full lips, afraid that staring into his eyes would betray her need. "Standing here doesn't mean I know what I want—well, I might want. It doesn't mean it's a good idea." She sounded like an idiot.

She had to get a grip on herself. If they were going to make love, she had to be able to look him in the eye. Cassie willed her gaze to his. That wasn't so hard. "I, um," What was she going to do? He would no doubt rock her world, but she knew herself. For her, sex would be a commitment with him, one she'd never get over. Her hand remained poised on his belly.

He lifted a questioning brow. "I lost at cards, remember. We don't have to."

This was the moment of decision. She'd just shared a bottle of ouzo and might not be thinking clearly, but she did want him. Not just for this first experience of making love, but because Apollo valued her. He found her capable and beautiful, and he believed in her. But was that enough of a motive to give herself to him?

Cassie waited for a reason to forge ahead or to warn her off. The prickle at the back of her neck didn't come, but she couldn't be sure. Her entire body tingled. She hesitated. Her body ached for him. Her moist hands shook and her brain refused to consider possible outcomes.

He dipped his head and nuzzled her ear. Something large and firm pushed against her belly. She didn't look, but guessed it must be his, um. Oh hell, she couldn't even think the word. This might be a mistake.

His mouth moved against her neck. "If you want to make love, it would be best if we removed your clothes."

"Clothes?" she sputtered, and jerked her hand away from his belly.

"They tend to get in the way," he whispered,

then unbuttoned her jeans and slid them down her hips.

She froze. "Uh, I. Uh." She stepped back, clutched her waistband, already low on her hips and showing the top of her white underwear. Was this how she wanted her first time? No romance, just a god willing to take her to bed? Desiring Apollo wasn't enough. She'd wanted more for herself. A commitment and marriage and this wasn't either. This would be sex. And then more sex and it would be fantastic, because it was Apollo. And damn it. She couldn't do it.

"No." she yanked up her jeans. "I can't"

He lifted his head. His mouth was tight. "Why not? It looked like you could a moment ago."

"I was wrong."

* * *

Apollo used every ounce of control not to take her. His member throbbed with need. She'd tempted him, and now she left him wanting. Did she mean to torment him and deny herself? He grumbled. Cassie was a virgin. Of course she'd hesitate, but he'd never expected her to flee from passion.

She backed away. "I'm sorry. I thought I could do this, but rejection was difficult enough when the relationships were superficial." She shook her head, tears glistening in her eyes. "Making love with you would mean everything. I know that now."

"And that's a problem?"

"It is for me. You won't stay, you can't. You're a god, for hell's sake."

"What does my being a god have to do with it? Mortal men leave women every day."

She swiped at her eyes with a shaky hand. "Exactly. I care for you too much to go further without a commitment."

His insides shook. No woman had urged him for a commitment in millennia. She couldn't be serious. "What are you asking, marriage?"

Cassie nodded, zipped up her jeans, and secured the button with a sniff. "Yes."

Apollo loved her, but marriage was another matter. He'd seen the arguments between Zeus and Hera. At times, Apollo pitied them both for joining. The constant fights had driven Zeus into the arms of many women, and Apollo didn't want that for Cassie. "It's a ridiculous idea."

"I know." Tears spilled the banks of her lashes. "Could you get dressed? You're distracting." She swiped at her eyes with her fingers.

He hated women's tears; more so the tears of this particular woman. That he was the cause irked him. It did more than irk, it crushed his heart like a vice. "Cassie, how can mortal vows hold a god?" He grabbed his slacks from the end of the bed.

She cleared her throat. "I suppose they can't. Is there no marriage between mortals and gods?"

"The gods marry. Zeus and Hera, Hades and Persephone, but none of those unions are ideal. Why would you wish to be condemned to such a life?" She couldn't really expect marriage, could she? He put one leg into his slacks and then the other.

"Is that how you see all marriage or just marriage with me?"

"Marriage is marriage." He shrugged, dismissing the idea and pulled up the slacks. "I am a god and you mortal. I love you. Isn't that commitment enough between us?" Hadn't she suffered enough as Cassandra that she insisted on more pain in this life? It made no sense.

Her lower lip trembled. "Not for me." She turned and shuffled to the door.

In his heart, he knew he could stop her with his promise of marriage and fill her with sweet words of conjugal bliss, but it would be the grandest lie he'd ever fabricated. The price to them both would be too high. "Where are you going?"

Cassie didn't turn to look at him, but opened the door. "To get my own room." She stood motionless as if waiting for him to say something. When he didn't, she said, "Will you do one thing for me?"

"If I'm able."

"Ask Zeus for help." Cassie walked through the door and closed it behind her.

Emotion wrestled within him. He loved Cassie

more than any woman, but was the feeling burning through his chest enough to ensure happiness? His gift of prophecy would have been useful at this moment. If their future had proven destructive, even Cassie would have to see the wisdom of enjoying each other for a time rather than promising for all time.

He slipped off his clothes, donned a toga and willed himself to the heavens and an audience with Zeus.

CHAPTER FIFTEEN

"How could Cassie doubt my commitment? I said that I loved her," Apollo grumbled as he strode through the entry to the court of the gods. He risked an audience with Zeus when he knew it was a mistake. All for love of Cassie.

Marble columns surrounded him, as rigid and imposing as his father. Apollo bowed before him. Zeus wore green shorts and an orange tank top with a straw hat perched upon his head. His father drummed his fingers on the arm of his golden throne in obvious annoyance. He must have plans. Apollo hoped that Zeus would want done with this and side quickly in his favor.

The seats flanking Zeus housed Hades, dressed in his usual drab garb, Aphrodite, the goddess of love, ensconced in pink gossamer, and his sister Artemis, draped in a traditional linen toga, with her quiver of arrows and bow resting at her feet. The rest of the seats were vacant. Not a good sign. Apparently there wasn't much interest in Earth's welfare.

Apollo breathed in, steeling himself to

convince them. "Great Zeus, thank you for giving ear to my request."

"What is it my son? After our last meeting, I didn't expect to see you so soon." His brow furrowed. "Is there a problem?"

"I ask for your mercy on Athens. Without my gift of prophecy, Hydra may well succeed and many mortals will die."

Hades thin gray lip curled. "Mortals die every day. It's the way of them."

"So it is." Zeus leaned back and steepled his fingers on his chest. "What is it to us that a few mortals die? Their lust for power is eternal and they think nothing of killing each other for gain."

Apollo didn't like the sound of this. Zeus had always held some regard for humanity. For Cassie and men's sake, he'd beg. "Would you punish all for the acts of a few? Have mercy on them. They don't see the evil and are like sheep being led to slaughter."

"Then let them be led." Hades pounded his bony fist on the arm of his bronze throne. "They are sheep that play at being men. If they will be led to destruction, it's their own doing."

Zeus slid his gaze to Hades. "There's wisdom in your words, but I'll hear out my son." His father leveled his sea-green gaze on him. "Tell me, Apollo, why should I act? The arrogance of men deserves retribution and they've created the means. Their pride blinds them. They are foolish and content in the illusion of safety. I hope you have more to justify your request than a few mortal lives."

His father had a point. Men trusted in science, not in the gods. Apollo had to take another tack. "If not for men, then for the city of Athens." Apollo lowered to one knee. "Your games are still held and your memory lives on through Mount Olympus."

"I do enjoy watching mortals at sport." Zeus nodded, a faint smile on his lips.

Hades glared with black eyes at Apollo. "These games celebrate mortal strength, not the gods. Is this the weak argument you place before great Zeus? You dishonor him and us."

Did Apollo have anything weightier than life to convince them? Life should have been enough, but to a god who lived forever it meant little. He tossed out the first idea that came to his mind. "Love is my reason."

"Love?" Aphrodite turned her beautiful face to him, her long blond hair brushing her shoulders. "I wish to hear more."

Artemis leaned forward. "You, my brother, in love? I find that almost impossible to believe." She smiled. "Tell me, who is it this time?"

Apollo winced at the accusation. He'd claimed love or lust for many a mortal, but this was far different. This emotion rooted in his breast and would never be dug out. "It's Cassandra, the woman I've reclaimed from the underworld and Hades."

"Oh yes, the wager." Zeus removed his hat and scratched his head. "How is that going?"

Lies to his father would not be tolerated, nor was it possible to deceive him for long. "She just told me she cares deeply for me."

Hades' creaky laugh reverberated over the marble walls. "Cares deeply? Yes, so much so that she refused to have you in her bed."

"It's a small matter. A difference of opinion," said Apollo. "If my gift of prophecy were reinstated, I could woo Cassie more effectively and win my wager. Hades seeks an unfair advantage from the loss of my gift."

Zeus stared down at Apollo from his throne high above the arena where the gods made requests and begged for mercy. Zeus hadn't been to Earth in thousands of years and had lost touch with the struggles of men. Mercy on behalf of mortals was doubtful. Apollo lowered himself to both knees. "Father, what can I do to gain your favor?"

Hades' grin darkened his features and turned evil. "Give up your love. That's a worthy sacrifice. You can't love a mortal more than Zeus."

Apollo's gut twisted in on itself. Zeus did demand loyalty above all and Hades knew it. Apollo hoped his father would see through his uncle's game.

"Do you love this woman?" asked his father. "Is she all that you'd hoped for and is she worth any price?"

"She is." Apollo might not have the gift of prophecy, but he could feel in his churning stomach that things were going in the wrong direction. Help saving the embassy was the last thing Cassie had asked from him. He couldn't give up. He cleared his throat. "Hades is a selfish monster, hoping to maneuver you so he wins the bet. Don't listen to him."

Zeus growled and sat up straight. Lightning flashed in his eyes. "Don't counsel me. I know Hades strives to win. I'm lord and will not be manipulated by god or man. You'll stay Apollo while I think on this."

"But Athens will fall."

"It may," said Zeus. "The Fates have decreed the attack in two days."

"Two days?" It might as well be two hours. He didn't even have a plan. "Then I ask for your answer now." Apollo knew he pushed the mightiest of all the gods. Not wise, but desperation won out over wisdom. Artemis shook her head at him.

The turbulent sea in his father's gaze rolled into angry dark green. A hurricane brewed in their depths. "I will not be commanded by my son and in my own court," he rumbled in a voice like thunder. Zeus slammed his staff on the marble floor and the entire temple shook. "Your arrogance rivals men's."

Apollo sunk low, hoping to dodge any stray thunderbolts. "Forgive me. My love for Cassandra causes me to act desperate."

The fire in his gaze cooled. "I will not separate you from this woman, but I won't aid you to destroy Hydra. I command that no help be given to Apollo." Zeus directed his fierce gaze on those present and they bowed under the weight of it. "I will be lenient to you this last time. Rather than send my lightning to level the city, I will return you to save it. If you can."

Apollo sucked in a breath. He didn't expect mercy. "Thank you."

Zeus raised his hand in warning, his eyes swirled dark. "That's not all. I return you, not with your gift of prophecy restored, but as a mortal."

Gasps echoed from the walls. Hade's blackened grin spread over his chalky face.

Apollo sunk to the ground and prostrated himself. "No. Please. They'll die."

"Then so be it," said Zeus.

Apollo's bones felt like they'd been filled with lead. He struggled to his feet.

Tears ran down his sister's pale cheeks and she ran to his side. Her blue eyes flashed. "Please Father. Can't you find some small gift to aid him? Hades drools over obtaining my brother's service." She pointed her slender finger at their uncle. "Look at the evil sitting beside you."

Zeus glanced to Hades. "He is what he is and always has been. I didn't make the wager with Hades. Apollo did."

Artemis opened her mouth to speak, but

Apollo pressed his fingers to her lips to silence her. "No use, sister. I'll take what comes, fight Hydra, and love Cassie as a mortal. If the Fates decree, I'll die with her."

* * *

In the morning, Cassie wasn't ready to face Apollo on an empty stomach. She'd bared her soul to him. He'd stared at her with his compelling blue eyes as if she'd asked for the impossible. He was a god, damn it. Marriage was within his power and he'd refused to commit to her. *Like all the other jerks.* It might be ridiculous, but it was what she wanted. Her mother had always told her it would be a mistake to settle for less in relationships and in life. *All or nothing.* "Have I chosen nothing?"

She shook off the depressing thoughts and left her room. Cassie walked two blocks to the market and stopped before a stand where a plump woman sold bread. The comforting scent of baked dough surrounded the stand. Her mouth watered. She'd barely eaten in two days. Freshly toasted pita beckoned.

A sharp prick at the base of her skull ruined the moment. Someone watched her. It was the same creepy feeling from the other day. Cassie scanned the busy market.

"Cassie." George closed the distance between them. "I've heard something. I'll tell you over coffee, but first, I must stop by a friend's shop. It'll only take a moment."

He leaned close. The sharp scent of oregano clung to him. "I was about to call your hotel. I can't believe my luck meeting you here."

The back of her neck itched and she rubbed it away with her fingers. Was someone following her? That's silly. Who would do that? "I'm the lucky one." She smiled. Finally, a break in this mess. Maybe they wouldn't need help from Zeus after all.

They strolled down a narrow street and turned right. "There." George nodded to a small, white building crowded between two beige apartments. Garlic braids hung in the window and a huge pot of rosemary sat outside. "Here we are. You must come inside and meet my friend. We go way back."

Cassie followed George inside the shop. Pungent aromas of herbs washed over her like a Mediterranean breeze. Oregano hung in clumps on the wall and rosemary branches were strewn on a table near the front. A pottery bowl loaded with lemons sat next to the cash register near the door. The fresh scents made her mouth water.

"Nic," called George to the back of a squat, balding man packing a box behind the register.

The man faced them. He was dark, with soft brown eyes. "You're here so soon. Have you brought me a customer?"

George laughed. "This is Cassie Priam, the American woman I told you about. We happened upon each other in the market. Imagine my surprise."

Nic's smile broadened. "Yes. A pleasure to meet you." He walked around the counter and took her hand. "George didn't tell me you were so beautiful. Come with me to the back for coffee and a little something to eat while my friend and I do business."

Cassie's neck prickled and the sensation shimmied down her spine. Something was off, but what? Maybe she was close to gaining information on Hydra?

Shrugging off the warning, she followed Nic as George brought up the rear. They made their way through a room overpowered by sweet lavender, jasmine and calendula hanging in bunches from the ceiling. A heavy table scattered with packets of rich spices looked ready for sale. The delicious scents argued with the tingle at the base of her head.

"I'm glad you were able to come so soon," said Nic as he maneuvered around a crate loaded with bottles of olive oil.

"It did work out well, didn't it?" said George from behind her.

Cassie didn't feel the "well" he referred to. The prickle progressed to needle pricks, but she couldn't see anything wrong. Her radar must be off, out of whack because she was still upset over Apollo.

Nic entered a tiny room with white plaster

walls, hugged on one end by a small wooden desk and a spindly chair. A skylight brightened the shabby space and made the room appear bigger.

"Our friends will congratulate you. Most impressive," said Nic as he moved to the desk.

"Thank you," chuckled George from behind her.

Pulling open a desk drawer, Nic retrieved a dark glass bottle and a rag. He popped open the lid, covered the opening with the cloth and tipped it over, soaking the rag "I'm glad you came when you did. If it had been an hour earlier, I wouldn't have had this." He nodded to the bottle in his meaty hand.

George took a spot just behind her and to her side. "Luck does smile on us."

Prickles raced down her back. Three warnings, and she decided to listen. "I need to go." She turned to leave.

George blocked her escape. Nic's thick arm grabbed her from behind and pressed her close to his bulk. She struggled, but he was too strong. "George, what are you doing? Help me!"

Nic covered her mouth and nose with the rag. "You're not going anywhere."

* * *

Apollo was furious. If he'd still had his powers, he would've throttled his spoiled half brother. All Hermes had to do was bring him to Athens near his hotel, but no, he'd taken a detour to Delphi. Showing Apollo his former greatness, rubbing his nose in his past glory. If by some miracle Apollo won the bet and gained Hades' hound, he'd turn the three-headed beast loose on Hermes. At least one set of jaws would bite a piece from his hide.

Hermes had taken his time, but finally deposited him on the outskirts of Athens. Apollo reached the hotel by late afternoon. Time wasted and they had none. He grumbled as he knocked on the door of her room. No answer. Was she just being stubborn or had she gone out? He trudged down the stairs to the front desk. They hadn't seen her since morning.

Something didn't feel right, and it was more than the blisters on his feet from walking. Cassie might have run into trouble. She'd lived a sheltered life. All she knew of danger came from human television and dreams. The girl had no real experience.

He left the hotel. The market had closed for the day. People milled about the cafés, but Apollo didn't see Cassie among them. Where could she have gone? Not to her father: she'd been too angry with him. Apollo's search brought him near Andromeda's home. He'd stop in for a moment and see if she might have an idea of where to look.

A thin young man with curly brown hair answered the door. "Come in. Come in. She told me to invite you if you came by. Andromeda hasn't stopped speaking of the handsome, blond god who visited. I'd know you anywhere."

Apollo entered. "I'm not a god, just a family friend." The truth of his words cut him. *Not a god. Mortal.* And he didn't care for the situation at all. Her humble home was clean and just as he recalled from his last visit. The young man had an expressive and friendly face and appeared to be about sixteen.

Andromeda nodded in her chair, her chin resting on her full bosom. The boy gently shook her awake. "He's here."

She jerked and her eyes blinked open. Apollo smiled at her, feeling that this woman's time on earth was ebbing away. He wished he'd seen her over the years, that he could turn back time and prolong her life. None of this was in his power. All he could offer was a brief visit.

"Apollo." She grinned, and then shook her hand at the lad. "Open a bottle of wine for us." Her crinkled eyes stared at him. "I'm glad you're here. The sight of you makes my heart sing with the memory of your grandfather."

"Your memories of him are good?"

"They sustain me in quiet moments. And this young man." The boy had returned and handed them full glasses, then set the bottle on the table beside the old woman. She smiled at the young man and he grinned back, genuine affection obvious between the two. She lifted her glass. "What troubles you?"

"Why do you think anything bothers me?"

Were his concerns so visible for all to see?

"I knew that look of your grandfather's. It always meant trouble."

"You're perceptive. There is trouble."

Her sparse gray brows lowered. "I'm old and likely can't do more than listen, but I can still do that."

"Anything you can tell me could help."

She settled a blanket over her lap and sat up straight. "Go on."

He set his glass on an end table. "I'm afraid that something might have happened to my fiancé. My gut tells me that Hydra has something to do with it."

Andromeda's gaze shifted to the boy and then back to Apollo. "Hydra? Filthy lot. They tried to convince Jason to join them. We talked about it and decided they were up to no good. He's a smart boy." She smiled at Jason and he beamed at her praise.

"You know of them?" Apollo perched on the edge of his chair in anticipation of any morsel of news.

Jason shrugged his slight shoulders. "I hear things. No one pays attention to me as I run errands. I'm always picking up things in the market and the shops for people. After I pay the money, they don't seem to notice if I stay and listen. It used to bother me, but then I started to learn things. It's not always a bad thing to be ignored."

"You've heard of Hydra?"

"Sure. They…well, I overheard this just last night." Jason leaned toward Apollo and lowered his voice. "An American woman is here and her father is some big deal in the US government. Hydra wants to take her hostage."

A cold ball of lard rolled in Apollo's gut. "An American? Did you hear the name?"

Jason tilted his head and scrunched his mouth. "Not sure, but her dad's the secretary of something. I remember that part."

Apollo's strength drained from him. "Priam?"

"That's it." Jason nodded. "I heard about it when I bought garlic from the herb shop a few streets over. Hydra's followers meet there sometimes."

"Will you show me?" Apollo jumped to his feet, adrenaline coursing through his limbs. This might be it. A feeling in his gut urged him to go.

Andromeda's gaze clouded with worry. "Take care, my boy."

"I will." Jason kissed her weathered cheek. "No fears. I'll be back soon."

CHAPTER SIXTEEN

As if propelled by an unseen force, Apollo strode through the streets and alleyways of Athens up a side street and down another, following the gawky young boy, Jason. He couldn't be more than sixteen, and was as thin as Poseidon's trident. Apollo's gut whispered that Cassie was near, not by godly ability, but a deeper sense. He hadn't expected that. Mortals did have gifts and he needed to make good use of them.

Music played from cafés, joyful tunes sounding over brick and stucco, mocking the reality of what lay ahead. Athens' destruction, and perhaps their own, loomed like storm clouds on the horizon.

"This is it." Jason hung back at the corner of the building and leaned against the wall. "See, closed like I said."

Apollo eyed the structure, careful not to get too close and appear overly interested to any bystander. "Is there a back way in?"

"Well, there was a door, but they closed it off. Now the only other way in is through the roof.

They have a window up top." He leaned closer to Apollo, and in a soft squeak he asked, "Are you planning to break in and rob the place? Because they only have dried parsley and garlic and not much money."

"No thievery. I've come for what's mine." Apollo didn't know that Cassie was inside, but the urge to search gnawed. He headed to the side of the building to gain a better look.

Jason tailed him, his light footsteps close on Apollo's heels. "What they got that's yours?" he whispered.

Apollo tuned his hearing to the shop and listened. Nothing. Mortal hearing did him no good. His jaw clenched. "Are you sure there's no one inside?"

Jason shrugged. "They're closed. That's all I can tell you."

"Is there a way up?" Apollo motioned to the roof. He'd scale the walls if need be.

"There's a ladder in back. They dry herbs on the roof and sometimes I haul them up for them."

"You're hard working." Apollo stalked toward the ladder.

"Need to make a living. I'm saving up for something." Jason hurried beside him.

"How old are you?" Apollo stared at the youthful face with a smudge of dark fuzz on his upper lip.

"Eighteen."

"What are you saving for, a motorcycle? I see

that's what many young people use to get around the city."

Jason grinned. "I plan to go to school in America and become a scientist."

"Do you?" Apollo lifted the wooden ladder, worn and gray. "And what kind of science are you interested in?"

"Nuclear physics. My teachers say I'm gifted, but I don't know about that." He shrugged. "I want to find a new source of power."

Apollo stopped beside a wall obscured by trees. Perfect. They'd be difficult to see from this spot. "I'm surprised."

"Why? Because I don't want to learn to blow things up, I can, you know—blow stuff up. That's why Hydra wanted me to join."

"Really." Apollo wedged the rickety, ladder against the building. "You're a man of many talents." He surveyed Jason. His eyes didn't lie. What kind of life had this boy led?

"Yeah, that's what Andromeda tells me." His large, dark eyes sparkled.

Apollo bounded up the ladder and Jason stood guard at the bottom. When he reached the top, Apollo spied the small window, only a foot square, impossible for a man of his size to squeeze through. Tension gripped his shoulders. No longer in possession of vision able to burn the hole larger or travel by thought to place him inside, he was forced to use human means for entrance. "Mortality is a curse," he muttered. Apollo waved at the boy and spoke low "Come up. I need your help."

Jason raced up the rungs and stood beside Apollo, staring at the skylight. "Yeah, you'll never get through that, but I fit. I'm skinny and small for my age. I've done it before."

"You have?"

"Sure. Sometimes I hand the dried herbs down through this window. And sometimes I drop to the floor instead of climbing down the ladder. It's faster."

"Are you willing to climb inside to find out if there's a woman in there?"

His wide mouth dropped open. "A girl? You mean the one they wanted to kidnap?"

Apollo nodded. He hoped and feared that was the case.

"Sure," said Jason, bright eyed and bouncing on his toes.

Apollo unlatched the covering and pushed aside the thick Plexiglas. The sun was setting and they both peered into darkness. A mass that looked like a rolled-up carpet lay in the center of the floor. It appeared soft—at least, softer than the ground.

"I'll try to land on that carpet to break my fall." Jason crawled through the small opening feet first. He struggled when he reached his shoulders, but forced passed and slipped down. Apollo heard a thud and then a muffled screech.

"What is it?" Apollo said in a loud whisper.

"I landed on the carpet and it's moving."

"See what it is." Desperation quickened Apollo's pulse and stared into the abyss.

A rustling wafted up from the darkness and then a grunt. "Ouch," from Jason.

"Apollo," screeched Cassie.

No sweeter sound had ever graced Apollo's ears. Thank the gods. He released a breath.

"Get—me—out," she growled.

* * *

Cassie's leg throbbed from the weight of the boy landing on it. There was sure to be a wicked bruise. She was lucky it wasn't broken. Apollo had carried her out of the building after the boy had let him in through the front door. Now she stretched out on his bed at their hotel with ice on her thigh. Apollo hadn't spoken to her most of the way, but the whites of his eyes shone red and he cleared his throat often. He carried her up the three flights of stairs and refused to let her out of his sight.

She'd been so relieved that Apollo had found her that she'd let go of her hurt and only now wondered if he'd met with Zeus. "Is your father helping us?"

"What?" Apollo glanced at her as he filled a new icepack. He'd sent Jason out to hunt up more ice.

"What did Zeus say?"

He dropped a cube on the floor. "Oh, nothing much."

A tingle crept along her neck. "I'm not buying that."

He flashed her a tight smile. "My father has chosen not to be involved."

"Ugh." Why did this not surprise her? In all of myth, when humanity needed the help from the gods, they dithered or were unavailable. "What excuse did he give you?"

"He didn't feel his involvement was needed."

"What would warrant his help? A meteor careening toward earth, resulting in total annihilation?" Cassie punched the mattress with her fist. "Zeus is an SOB."

Apollo shrugged, closed the ice pack and placed it gently on her thigh, midway between her knee and her hip. "How does it feel?"

"Numb, thanks to the ice and aspirin." She adjusted her leg and made a careful stretch. "Yep, it will be much better by morning. Stiff maybe, but I'll be able to walk on it." Cassie rubbed above the swollen spot with her fingers. "Where did you find this kid?"

"Jason works for an old friend. He's trustworthy and bright. The boy longs for an education in America, but he'll struggle to pay for his dream." Apollo sighed heavily, his blue eyes shifting to inky. "He knows something about Hydra's plans and I believe him."

Cassie sat up. "What has he told you, other than where to find me?"

"That was luck, but I'll ask him more when he

returns."

A knock on the door, and Jason entered with a bowl. "You know, we don't use ice much. I had to go to one of the big American hotels to get this."

"I appreciate it. Thanks," said Cassie. "It *almost* makes up for your landing on me."

"He stared at her with repentant brown eyes. "Sorry, I didn't know you were the lumpy carpet."

"Is that what I looked like?"

Jason grinned. "Yep. You don't think I would've jumped on you if I'd known you were a girl, do you?"

"I suppose not." She smiled back at him.

Apollo sat on the bed beside Cassie and motioned for Jason to take the chair by the door. His brow creased. "I need to ask you a few questions. Aiding us may be dangerous. Are you willing?"

"I've lived on the streets most of my life." He crossed his arms over his thin chest. "I was in trouble from the moment I refused to join Hydra, more after I agreed to take you to the shop. Too late now."

He was right. If anyone saw him at the herb shop tonight, Hydra would take care of him. Cassie doubted they'd show leniency because of his age. She felt a ping of discomfort for the boy's situation.

Apollo rested his arms on his thighs and stared at the boy. "I need more information. We've thwarted part of their plan, but they'll move forward regardless. Is there anything else you can tell me?" He spoke in a soft voice and didn't push for an answer.

Jason scrunched his face and looked up at the ceiling in obvious thought. "They want to blow up a government building, take hostages, shoot a few people to make a point, and then do other stuff."

"What...other stuff?" said Apollo.

"Take over the world is what they told me, back when they pushed me to join them."

Apollo didn't laugh.

Cassie wished it was a joke, but the look on the boy's face was serious. "How do they plan to do that?" she said.

He shrugged his skinny blue t-shirt-clad shoulders. "I'm not on the inside, so I don't know details, just what I hear around."

"Is that everything?" Apollo wiped his hands on his thighs.

"They may have changed their scheme, but they'd planned to bomb something in Athens."

Cassie flinched, and then groaned from the pain of movement. "I won't do that again." She rubbed her leg. "Do you have a time?"

"Sure. They told this guy George all about it while I picked up fennel seeds in the herb store. I ducked around a bunch of hanging garlic and listened. They didn't notice me and talked for another hour. I knew Andromeda would wonder what took so long, but I couldn't leave and get caught listening."

"Of course not," said Cassie. Smart boy. *George?* It had to be that damn traitor of a friend.

Apollo clenched and unclenched his fists and stared at the floor. "We need to know how they mean to get into the embassy."

"Embassy?" Jason sat up. "I never said it was the embassy, but they did say that was a possible target. Wow. They mentioned the seventeenth of this month."

"The seventeenth." Cassie's stomach roiled. "That's when the officials meet in Athens to negotiate with Hydra. Are you sure?"

Apollo leveled a glacial blue gaze on her. "He's right. The attack is fated for two days time."

Jason cocked his head toward Apollo. "Fated? Whatever. That must be the plan. Wait until they have a bunch of prisoners in one place and then take them hostage."

Apollo nodded. "Wise move."

"What?" said Cassie, her head jerking toward Apollo. "You can't agree with this."

"No, but it's not a bad plan."

Cassie sat back against the pillows. "No, it's not." *Damn. My dad will be there.*

Jason lifted from the chair and headed for the door, but Apollo stopped him. "You can't leave."

"But Andromeda. She'll be worried if I don't come home."

"You live there?" asked Cassie.

"It beats the street. I do things for her and she lets me stay. It's a good trade."

Apollo handed him the phone. "Tell her I have a job for you and you'll be back tomorrow."

"A job?" he said, punching in the number. "What does it pay?"

Apollo glanced at Cassie and she nodded, knowing what he intended. She had some savings and they'd work it out. Apollo was a god, after all.

Apollo then looked to the boy. "If you can help us and we succeed, a ticket to the United States and means to attend a university."

Jason's eyes bugged out and he shouted, "Yes!"

Cassie giggled at his excitement. "Well, if we get through this, I'm going to need your age and legal name for the passport."

"My name?" He still bounced with excitement on his spindly legs. "Mignon. Jason Mignon."

Apollo's shoulders shook. He leaned back on the bed and laughed, tears streaming from his eyes and ran into his ears.

"What's so funny?" asked Cassie, bewildered.

He wiped at his eyes and gasped a breath. "Mignon. I have a *minion*."

CHAPTER SEVENTEEN

Morning came too soon. Cassie had taken the bed, Apollo the chair and Jason had nabbed a spot on the floor. Not that any of them had slept much; they were up most of the night planning against the attack scheduled in just two days. Cassie had given up on the ice. Her stiff leg argued for staying immobile and the bruise turned ugly purple-black with a knot of muscle in the middle. Yep, not pretty at all. Her mom would faint when she saw it.

Apollo hunched in the chair over his thoughts, his linen jacket a mass of wrinkles. He looked tired. She didn't know a god could be affected by anything. Maybe it was worry.

They'd decided late last night to give her dad one more try. He had to see reason. Moving the meeting's location might be enough to avert disaster. She'd called and left her dad a message to contact her pronto.

If that didn't work, they had a back-up plan; setting up a strike themselves and closing the embassy before the dignitaries arrived. Jason would be instrumental in that effort constructing bombs. She didn't agree with violence, but a well-placed explosion, just to blow smoke and draw attention, would do no real harm and close the embassy.

Apollo prepared to purchase the necessary items. Jason continued the youthful slumber of most teen boys. It would take a bomb to wake him.

Cassie slipped into her shoes and limped to the chair. "Are you ready?"

"Just looking over the list Jason gave us last night. It's just a few common ingredients that we should be able to find easily, but not all from the same location. I wouldn't want to be caught before we execute."

A shudder ran over her. "I don't want to be caught at all. I can see the headlines now, 'Secretary's daughter arrested in embassy bombing plot'. My mom would be mortified. I'd go to prison and it would ruin my dad's career. So yes, lets purchase from as many locations as we can. Maybe we can fund Jason into some shopping."

"He'll enjoy it." Apollo's lips formed an uneasy smile.

"I think so. He spent half the night telling me about how he'd learned to build simple explosive devises from a guy that escaped from prison in Africa. The man wanted to keep up his skill. He took Jason under his wing and they built bombs together." She lowered her voice. "Jason has been working with explosives for two years and he's kept it hidden from Andromeda all this time. He's never told anyone until now."

Apollo cocked his head. "I missed this. Must have gone for more ice. Andromeda never would have allowed any of that if she'd known. How well did the bombs work?"

"Well enough to fill their boat with fish in the middle of the night."

"Have they tested in anything but the ocean?"

"I'm not sure." Cassie rubbed her leg above the bruise through her jeans. "They can't have tried too often or they would've been caught."

"But the boy has gained Hydra's attention. They knew of his skills."

"Yes. We'll need to learn more about that." Cassie had a horrible thought. "You don't think Jason had anything to do with bombing the train stations?"

Apollo crinkled his brow. "No, but the man who taught him might be involved."

That sounded more likely. The boy had turned Hydra down and didn't want to be part of their sick plans.

Jason shifted in the corner, his arms tucked under his head for a pillow. He stretched, blinked, and then sat up, rubbing the sleep from his eyes. "Do we need to get going?" He yawned and laid back on the blanket. "Just five more minutes, I'll be awake then."

Apollo nudged him with his foot. "There isn't time. Every minute counts."

Jason groaned and pushed himself up again. "Okay, okay. You act like Andromeda. By the way, I need to call her. She'll be needing me to fix her lunch later."

"We'll stop in on our way," said Apollo.

Cassie's phone buzzed and vibrated on the table next to the bed. She snatched it up. "Dad!" She listened to him shoot out information. "That's fantastic? When? Yes, that's wonderful. Congratulations!" Her father had spoken so fast in his excitement she barely caught it all. "We were hoping to see you. This afternoon will be great."

Cassie glanced to Apollo. "My dad wants to have lunch with us."

Apollo nodded.

"Okay, we'll see you at one." She ended the call.

"You won't believe it." Cassie felt giddy with joy and wiggled as she sat on the bed. "The meeting with Hydra is cancelled. They've reached an agreement. Dad said they're all leaving. He didn't want to get into it on the phone, but said he'd meet us at a cafe in Athens for lunch."

"They worked something out with Hydra?" said Apollo, speculation in his eyes.

"I guess so."

"No bombs?" asked Jason.

Apollo smiled at the boy. "It appears not."

Jason fell back on his mound of blanket. "Then

I can sleep?"

"No," said Apollo. "I'd feel better if we bought supplies, just in case. Something is just not right about this."

Cassie didn't want to agree with him, but prickles stung the back of her neck during her dad's call.

* * *

Apollo couldn't shake the dread pummeling his gut. Jason walked ahead, showing them the locations for the items on the list. Cassie chattered with the boy and tugged at her dark hair. Her smile stretched tight, her voice pitched higher than usual. She looked nervous. They all were. An unusual experience for him, he usually didn't worry over much. As a god, he could handle most situations easily. But now?

They each took part of the list, and in a few hours they'd gained a ravenous appetite and enough materials to level a city block.

"We need to stow this someplace," said Cassie, shifting the sacks in her arms.

Jason piped up. "We can leave everything at Andromeda's house. After I take care of her, I'll work on a device."

"Good idea." Apollo took a sack from Cassie and added it to his burden. "Then no time wasted while Cassie and I meet with her father."

"Yeah," said Jason, snatching a sack from Cassie. "I'll have to be careful. If I know

Andromeda, she'll question me about what I've been up to, but I can avoid telling her much. She's worse than two mothers."

Cassie grinned. "Oh, I don't know about that."

Apollo chuckled. Cassie's mother could change his mind.

They hurried through the labyrinth of streets to Andromeda's house. Apollo knew that she'd taken Jason in three years ago when she'd found him nibbling the food she'd intended for her cat. Jason hadn't told them where he'd lived before that or how he'd happened to be in Athens. His parents had lost track of him. Apollo's jaw hardened. How could parents leave a young boy to fend for himself in this city? The pain that shadowed Jason's eyes when he spoke of finding them gone warned him off the subject. In time, perhaps Jason would trust them enough to share the rest of the story.

Andromeda welcomed them into her home. "Jason, I thought Apollo might have stolen you from me, like his grandfather ran away with my heart," she teased.

"That was fifty years ago." Apollo leaned closer to Cassie and lowered his voice. "You hadn't been reborn yet."

Cassie rolled her eyes at him and then handed the woman a loaf of bread and a bottle of good wine. "It's a pleasure to meet you."

Andromeda graciously accepted the token and handed it to Jason. "Thank you. And you must be the reason for Apollo's need to take Jason from me yesterday. I'm glad that they found you." She took Cassie's hand. "You remind me so much of myself, back when I was a pretty young thing."

Apollo shrugged. "I have a weakness for a certain type."

"You rascal." Andromeda grinned at Apollo, her crinkled eyes full of joy. "If you're like your grandfather, your weakness is for all pretty women." She focused on Cassie again, "Oh don't mind me, dear. His grandfather was a bit of a rogue, but I'm sure this one has learned from his mistakes." She winked at Apollo.

Apollo slipped his arm around Cassie's waist and drew her close. "When you find what you're looking for, you stop searching." The truth of his words warmed his heart. Cassie *was* all he'd ever hoped for—brave, intelligent, beautiful and she made him laugh. Now if he could only find a way to convince her of his love and commitment, they might know happiness.

"True enough," said Andromeda, lowering her slight frame into a worn painted chair.

Jason scurried away with the gift and their supplies.

"I'm sorry for keeping Jason from you, but by the time we found Cassie and returned to the hotel, it was late," said Apollo, taking a seat on the couch beside Cassie.

"Oh, I imagine he finds running with you young ones more entertaining than staying with an old goat like me. He's such a kind boy and he's had it rough." Her mouth turned down and she shook her head. "Those parents of his were no good."

"He was lucky to have found you," said Cassie.

"I'm blessed. I don't know what I'd do without the boy, but he's growing into a man. He'll leave soon and find his own way in the world."

"And what will you do?" asked Apollo, concerned for his old friend.

"Oh, I expect I'll take a place near the ocean and watch the sunset."

She had a far away look for a moment. "I wish I could've gone to America and seen my brothers again, visit my family, see their children and grandchildren." She pulled her gaze back and clucked her tongue. "I'm too old now and my health is poor. That wish is past."

"Have you given up on your dreams?" said Cassie.

"Dreams are cheap, it's reality I can't afford. The trip would be too much for me."

Apollo wanted to wrap Andromeda in his arms and will her to America, give her the gift of her family and some joy, but being mortal, he had no such power and it stabbed at his ribs.

Jason entered the room and stood beside Andromeda. She looked up at the boy and wrapped her arm around his waist. "Jason is family enough for me."

The boy's dark brows knitted together. "Did they tell you? I won't go if it'll make things too hard for you."

She shook her gray head. "What are you talking about?"

Jason knelt at Andromeda's side and pressed his palm to her cheek. "I'm going to a university in America. I'll have the life I've always wanted."

"Oh Jason, it's what I've hoped for." she murmured, and then buried her face in her withered hands and cried "I'm so happy."

The boy wrapped her in his thin arms. His shoulders shook as he lowered his head to hers. Finally, they turned to Cassie and Apollo. Andromeda's eyes shone with moisture and appreciation. "What did we ever do to deserve the two of you and such kindness?"

Apollo cleared his throat. "You were kind to a young man fifty years ago, and he remembers you with fondness."

The visit was short, but valuable. Apollo's time on Earth and the relationships he'd formed made life worthwhile. The gods had forgotten this and the loss had cankered their souls. He gazed at Cassie. She was a gift he'd treasure for as long as he lived—if he lived.

CHAPTER EIGHTEEN

The sun shone like a ball of yellow butter—glorious, especially after their visit with Andromeda. Nothing lifted Cassie's spirits like helping someone. She hoped lunch with her dad would continue along the same positive lines. He'd sounded excited on the phone. Negotiations must have gone well.

Cassie and Apollo neared the café. Tables were scattered outside under a navy canvas awning. People milled about, some seated and conversing, others laughing. Yes, this had turned out to be a great day. She spied a young couple at a small table, their heads bent close together and their eyes locked on each other in obvious longing. A jealous twinge pricked her heart. She wanted a relationship like that. She stole a glance at Apollo as they walked. The twinge expanded to an ache. He'd refused to commit.

Her stomach knotted at the thought and her eyes burned. Apollo was an arrogant, meddling excuse for a god. After spending hours tied up in that musty herb shop, she'd figured something out. Apollo would never marry her.

And she loved him, damn it.

He strode beside her with the fluid motion of an athlete. His golden hair brushed his broad shoulders, making it all the more striking against his white shirt. Had she made a huge mistake by forcing marriage? Apollo wasn't perfect, but he cared for her. He showed up when she needed him. Was she a fool to pass up a relationship with him when it was all she wanted?

Cassie swallowed her regret. She was a big coward. Her relationships with men had gone nowhere, but she'd healed—mostly. Apollo said that his love was his commitment. Why wouldn't she accept that? It was more than any man had offered her, and he was more than a man. The love of a god, a man who wouldn't easily lie to her, and all she wanted, and she'd flushed it because of her pride. She'd made a mess of it.

Apollo gave her father's name to the hostess and they were led to a private room in the back of the café.. Cassie picked out the secret service agents at an adjoining table. "Hi," she said, and gave the three men a nod. They sat erect and ready, like guard dogs licking their chops.

They moved to put Apollo through a body check. "Arms above your head and legs apart, sir."

Apollo leveled an indignant glare at the agent. Cassie had seen that look just before John's hair took fire. At any moment Apollo might shrivel them to jerky.

"Is this necessary?" said Cassie. "Dad, you know Apollo."

Her dad called them off with a gruff, "Stand down." He nodded at the empty seats at the linen-covered table. "Of course, your young man."

She winced at her dad's words and wished they were true. Apollo might have been her man if she hadn't demanded the impossible from a god. Cassie sat beside her dad and Apollo claimed the seat next to her.

Cassie shoved away the painful thoughts and focused on hearing what happened with Hydra. "Is it over?" she said. "You reached an agreement?"

"We'll talk after we eat," said her dad. "I want to enjoy this meal with my daughter. I take it Apollo is up to speed on how things run, security, all of that."

She gave a nervous laugh. "He is now."

"Well son, politics is an education. I'll be leaving in the morning for home. We succeeded. Negotiations went entirely our way. I can't discuss details. No offense young man, but you understand." The secretary glanced from Apollo to his menu. "Nice work, I'd say."

"Yes," said Apollo. "I hope you're still taking precautions. You can't trust someone who would kill innocents."

Her father stared up from his menu. "Oh, I never said we trusted them. It's the old adage, keep your friends close and your enemies in your vest pocket."

"Dad likes to change the old adage up a bit and make it his own," she said. Something didn't feel right. Maybe it was the subject they discussed or the concern wrinkling Apollo's brow.

"I've a full day before leaving Greece," said her dad. "How about we order and I find out more about this young man. Who are you, exactly?" He lowered his brows and waited.

Cassie twirled a lock of her hair between her damp fingers. Why was she nervous? Her dad was about to interrogate a god. Maybe piss him off and end up with his gray hair singed off, nothing to worry about.

"The man who loves your daughter." Apollo snagged her hand. His was bone dry, hers wasn't.

"Humph," grunted her dad. "And…"

Damn. This was a disaster in the making and she couldn't sit by and do nothing. "We're dating," blurted Cassie. Her dad didn't know who he was messing with and she didn't want him to find out.

"Dating?" Apollo cocked his head and gazed at her. "I'd say it's more serious than that."

"Is it?" asked her father leaning forward, his eyes intent. "How serious? Are we talking marriage?"

Why not rip her heart out and set fire to it? She did not want to have this conversation. And what game was Apollo playing? He refused to commit. *Please, let this all be over.* "Dad, I'd rather we didn't get into it just now."

"This is a perfectly good subject for us to discuss, and since we have a little time, I suggest we get to it." He glared at Apollo. "How serious?"

Sweat trickled down her sides moistening her white gauze blouse. Torture, that's what this was. Emotions swirled in her tightening chest, none of them comfortable.

Apollo squeezed her hand. "I haven't asked your daughter to marry me, but I want to share my life with her."

Her dad's lips pinched together. "I hope you're talking marriage."

The server arrived, stifling the discussion. She poured red wine into their glasses and her dad waved her away. "Are you here to ask my blessing?"

Apollo paused.

Cassie wanted to yank her sweaty hand from Apollo's grip and run. Why didn't he just say no, never, not going to happen and be done with it? Why was he prolonging her humiliation?

He reached into the pocket of his slacks and captured her with his striking azure gaze. "Cassie, I'd be honored if you'd be my wife."

"What?" She couldn't have heard him right. That had to be her imagination. Apollo pulled a gold band from his pocket, lifted her trembling hand and slipped the ring onto her finger. "For now and forever." He pressed his lips to her knuckles.

Cassie couldn't tear her gaze from Apollo's face and the tender look in his eyes. "Really?" she murmured. "But I thought…"

"I was a fool," he interrupted.

Her vision blurred with pooling moisture. "What changed your mind?"

"You." The edges of his mouth tilted up. "Nothing exists without you, not for me."

"Hold on." Her dad's voice floated to her over the table. "I'd like to know more about you first." He raked Apollo with a harsh glare. "What is it that you do?"

"Do?" Apollo answered.

"Yes, work, career, how do you intend to support my daughter?" The lines around her dad's mouth deepened.

"I don't work," Apollo said without apology.

Cassie knew that wouldn't fly with her dad. He expected husbands to be responsible and have a solid future.

A low growl resonated in her dad's throat and he stared at Apollo a long while. "You must do something."

Apollo shrugged. "I play a number of instruments."

Her dad's face blazed red. He lifted his napkin from his lap and threw it down on the table with force. "Cassie, a musician?" he roared. "He's unemployed. Where do you find them? The last young man actually showed up outside of my car trying to get a job at the FBI. I told him off."

Cassie perked up and the back of her neck tingled. "You did what?"

He shook his graying head. "Oh, there's been a slew of these kind, opportunists sniffing for money. Eric was the worst of that lot. If he hadn't backed off, I would have put the fear of the all mighty in him."

Apollo nodded. "I'm in agreement with you. Some of the people she's dated. They weren't worth the price of the soil they were crafted from."

Cassie stared between the two. "But I was young. I just wanted to have a boyfriend and have fun. Dating wasn't serious, it never got to that point."

"Not with those derelict rejects," grumbled her dad. "I had to scare one away by sending the agents to his door to interrogate him. He never called again."

Cassie's mouth dropped and her stomach felt like she'd swallowed a bag of rocks. "It was you? Daddy, you didn't get rid of everyone I went out with, did you?"

He leaned back in his seat. "Not all. A few took off without my help, but the majority needed at least a stern talking to before they'd leave you alone. I saw to that." He smiled and rested his hands over his belly in a manner, suggesting that he was proud of himself.

"You didn't?" she breathed.

"Princess." He sat up and patted her free hand

resting on the table. "It's my duty as your father to protect you from riffraff. None of those young men were worthy of you. And now you consider a proposal from this pretty boy with no ambition and no job." He scowled at Apollo. "Every few months another flake to brush off."

Apollo's jaw clenched. "I don't work because I have no need. I have more than sufficient means to care for Cassie. She'll want for nothing."

Her dad sneered. "We'll see. You do understand that I'll have to check you out. I can't be too careful with my only daughter."

Apollo's nostrils flared. Cassie feared his temper would ignite and her dad would be hanging from the ceiling fan any moment.

Cassie hadn't recovered from Apollo's marriage proposal before her dad admitted he'd ruined her social life, and stripped away her self-esteem. She continued to stare at the two of them, her lips parted ready to speak, yet unable to do more then grunt.

"Cassie?" her father growled. "I haven't given you my blessing on this young man. Don't do anything rash."

Cassie's mouth trembled. "I've lost my appetite. Apollo and I have to make arrangements to fly home." She stood, needing to escape this nightmare. She'd had no idea that her dad had gone to such lengths to scare off men. Her reality imploded. Struggling to hold herself together among the thrash of emotions pouring in, she sucked in a breath. "I'd expect this from Mom, but not you. It's my life and I'll do what I want with it."

Apollo took her arm. "Mr. Secretary."

Her dad didn't get up. Cassie's eyes welled with tears. She broke free from Apollo, racing from the café and out into the open air.

Apollo caught up to her. "Your father will see reason. He's no worse than Zeus."

She stopped walking, shocked by his comment. "Oh, like that's supposed to make me feel better. Zeus is a freakin' monster. Ugh. All this time, I'd thought there was something wrong with me. It was bad enough when you ran off a few men, but this betrayal by my dad..." Cassie stomped her foot. "I knew he was controlling, and he often treated me like a little girl, but I had no idea he was this manipulative."

"You should talk to him."

"Why? I'm a grown woman and the damage is done." Anger and adrenaline sizzled in her muscles and she had to move. Cassie sped through the winding streets as she vented. "Why talk to him? It's not as if he'll change. And I thought my mom was impossible."

Apollo grabbed her by the elbow and slowed her escape. "He's your father. I don't agree with his methods, but he's your family. Nothing on Earth or in the heavens will ever change that."

Cassie looked into his eyes and saw truth shining back at her. "Maybe not, but I'm still angry with him."

"Your father loves you and didn't want those men to hurt you."

"I might have hurt them instead. We'll never know. I could've realized who was good for me, maybe gained strength and stood up for myself before now against my parents. That might have come hard, but it would've been worth it."

Sadness shadowed his gaze. "It was never my intention to…"

She shook off his apology. "You wanted to protect me and I guess my dad thought he was doing the same, but I need you to understand why this upsets me."

"Of course I understand. I have my own controlling, power-wielding father. Remember?"

"How can I forget?" Cassie wished she had argued with her dad more; expressed her needs and held her ground when it mattered to her over the years. "Have you ever gone up against Zeus?"

He pressed his lips into a firm line. "We butt heads continually. I believe he expects it. Zeus admires his children for standing up to him. Not that punishment for doing so isn't swift and, at times, severe."

* * *

They walked at a calmer pace along the busy street, and though Cassie's nails no longer dug into Apollo's arm, she did mutter under her breath on occasion. It might not be the best time, but he needed her answer. Everything hinged on this, the wager, but above that, life with his beloved. "Cassie?"

"Huh?" She kept her focus on the street as they strolled.

Apollo needed her full attention. If she accepted him, she must do so with full awareness. "Do you love me?"

Her head lifted, her dark hair a covering of black silk over her shoulders. Confusion fogged her gaze. "Yes."

He released a breath in relief. "You accept my proposal, then?"

Her violet eyes widened, framed by thick black lashes. "Oh! Sorry. I meant to say yes, but my Dad." She shook her head. "Not going there." Her tongue darted out between her lips. "I know you don't agree with a mortal wedding, and I understand why. A vow from a god should be enough for any girl. I'd rather accept your commitment of love, and this ring, than any legal paper."

"That's enough for you?"

She nodded, proof of her feeling for him apparent in her tearful gaze.

"Will you take vows with me?" he said. "Not in a mortal ceremony, but binding."

Her chin trembled. "Oh, yes. When?"

"Is now too soon?"

* * *

Acres of forest lay below the Acropolis. Apollo had chosen a spot in the dense wood beside an ancient olive tree. No temple of cold stone hewn by mortal hands for this most sacred moment. He would have sun on his face and birds singing to mirror the love in his heart.

They stood together inches apart and face to face. Her beauty rivaled nature. "Are you sure?" He searched Cassie's face for signs of doubt.

A smile lit her face and brightened her eyes. "Positive."

Apollo removed the ring from her hand and held it up to her. The delicate gold band carved in the form of a laurel wreath had been the sign of marriage to the gods, and now it would be the symbol between he and Cassie. His throat constricted with emotion and he struggled to speak. "My love, this ring symbolizes our eternal vow. Before the gods, I promise to love you for eternity."

Cassie swiped at tears spilling over the banks of her lashes as he took her hand. "I don't know what to say," she sniffed.

"Speak from your heart."

"I've waited for a lasting relationship. When you offered your love I was too afraid and stubborn to accept until now. I love you Apollo, more than I have words."

He slid the golden wreath on her finger, wrapped her in his arms and covered her mouth in a sealing kiss.

CHAPTER NINETEEN

Her wedding would never hold up in court and her parents would be livid.

Cassie didn't care.

In her heart, she knew they were joined by love. If a god had to bless the ceremony for it to count, well, she had that covered too.

A gentle breeze rustled the olive leaves on the tree. The branches swayed. Cassie stood in the shelter of her husband's arms and sighed into the crisp white fabric of his shirt. His sweet scent made her mouth water and she lifted her gaze to take him in. "Apollo." She swallowed. "Are we, um. Will we...you know." Her cheeks burned.

He brushed his lips over hers. "Make love?" he whispered against her mouth.

At the moment, there was nothing she wanted more. She nodded, afraid her voice would squeak and she'd stammer. She pressed her cheek against his chest and felt the rumble of his laughter.

"I long for you." He nuzzled the top of her head. "Our hotel is near."

Excitement danced through her like sparks of

electricity. "We have hours before we have to meet at Andromeda's."

"We do." He hugged her. "But eternity will never be enough time with you."

When they arrived at his hotel room, Cassie stared at the bed looming before her, draped in pale yellow fabric.

"Cassie." Apollo came up behind and slipped his arms around her. "Don't be afraid. This first time may be a bit uncomfortable, but I'll be gentle."

Her heart pinged and her mouth went dry. She turned in his arms to face him. "I'm not afraid, just nervous."

He smiled, his eyes soft as the summer sky. How did curving his lips give her courage? It did. Apollo cupped one hand around her nape and cradled her head. He feathered kisses first along her hairline and then her closed eyes. She hungered for her mouth to be next. She licked her lips in anticipation.

He took her mouth, gentle strokes of his tongue gaining entrance, each swipe an artful caress and a promise of more to come. She leaned into him, her hands on his firm chest. The steady rhythm of his heart beat strong beneath her fingers. He was real. Flesh and blood—and hers.

She joined in the kiss. He groaned against her lips and deepened his efforts. Nervousness dissolved with each moment giving way to need. Her jeans were too tight. Her white gauze blouse restricted against her heated skin.

He broke off the kiss and she moaned in protest. His wet mouth moved to the tender spot on her neck. Her knees buckled. She grabbed onto his shoulders to stay upright as her head fogged and her body tingled.

"Off." Did she say that?

Clothes fell to the floor. No embarrassment, just desire. He pressed her back into the mattress burning a trail down her body with his mouth. He stroked, kissed, caressed with tenderness and hunger. It brought back the dreams of his seduction, stoking her passion with each touch. Her hands slid down his muscled back. Her core pulsed. She couldn't get close enough to him, needing more than skin to skin. Heat built inside her from a smolder to a scorching blaze. He entered her slowly.

Did she scream?

Not from pain. A moment of discomfort gave way to a flood of pleasure that ebbed and flowed and consumed her in waves. She floated in a sea of sensation. Each kiss and caress drove her to know his body as he claimed hers. Her lips traveled over his chest. The sweet, salty taste of him was addictive and she needed more.

He quickened his pace and took her higher. She dug her fingers into his back and hung on. She thought she'd break apart. Barriers gone, exquisite joy burst through her. Tears streamed from her eyes and dampened her hair. She couldn't contain the love filling her and breaking free.

He pushed deeper, a relentless drive that went beyond owning her body. He demanded her soul. Release upon release wracked her until she shattered, again and again, until he owned every inch of her.

After, he gathered her to the warmth of his body and looked down at her, concern wrinkled his brow. "Are you alright? I didn't hurt you, did I?"

"No. I just…" She sniffed and peered through bleariness at the man she'd waited for. "I love you so much. I didn't…I never imagined."

Apollo ran his fingers along her jaw. She blinked to focus and saw a tear glistening on his cheek. "No words, beloved." He kissed her.

He was right. Their hearts had already spoken.

CHAPTER TWENTY

Three hours later, Apollo and Cassie, still flushed from passion, strolled to Andromeda's home. He drank Cassie in. Redness from his beard stubble shone on the tender skin of her face and neck. Other proof of his ardor hid beneath her clothes. Each time he took possession of her, his desire deepened. He'd never be sated. She'd wrapped herself around his heart and he'd keep her there. Apollo wished for days rather than hours to enjoy each other. Later, after they'd made arrangements for Jason's trip to America, then he'd make love to Cassie in a manner befitting his skill.

Apollo wrapped on the door. They waited and again he knocked. No answer came. His gut turned in on itself. Something was wrong. He opened the door and walked in with Cassie close behind. The sight that met them twisted his nerves all the way down his spine. A painted chair turned on its side. A broken wine bottle on the floor, its contents poured out in a red pool on the brown tile. "Andromeda," he called and strode by broken glass littering the ground. He'd seen this before; the signs of struggle by those forcibly taken from their homes.

"Jason?" called Cassie. She retrieved a blanket from the floor and placed it in Andromeda's chair.

"They've been taken," said Apollo, his eyes scanning, hoping to find a hastily scrawled note.

"They?" asked Cassie, pulling at a lock of her flowing hair. "Who would kidnap them?"

"It must be the group working with Hydra." He rummaged through paper on the dining table. "There's no other explanation." If he'd retained prophecy, then he would've seen this and his friends wouldn't be in danger. He looked up to the ceiling and mentally implored his father: *Now would be a fine time to reinstate my gifts.*

"But why? Jason had refused to work with them and he's just a kid."

No response from Zeus, but Apollo clung to hope. He glanced back to Cassie. "They must need him. Jason is a useful young man, skilled with explosives."

"Maybe they didn't take him," she said twisting her hair until it looked like an inky cord of rope. "He might have gotten away."

Apollo shook his head. "No. They'd only take Andromeda to force Jason's cooperation."

Footsteps sounded from the back of the small house. "Jason?" said Cassie.

"I thought you'd return." A dark-haired man trained an automatic weapon on Apollo. Four other men, two carrying similar guns, strode into the cramped space.

"George," snarled Cassie. "You rotten bastard."

The man nodded to her. "A pleasure."

Apollo wouldn't chance Cassie's life by fighting them. He was mortal and five against one wasn't the best odds.

"You escaped from us once, Cassie, but not again," said George. "Tie them up, him first." He tossed a coil of rope to a freckled young man. George leveled the gun on Cassie as he spoke to Apollo. "Give us any trouble and she's dead."

Freckleface moved behind Apollo. "Hands behind your back."

Apollo glared at George, but complied. Trapped by mortals, he ground his teeth in frustration. When he was able, he'd thrash the lot of them. Freckles bound his wrists together.

A man, the shape of a brick, yanked a pack off of his back and reached inside, pulling out a glass bottle and a cloth. Cassie's eyes widened and she backed away.

A skinny young man grabbed her arms from behind. "Hold still. It won't hurt."

She struggled and he shook her hard. Cassie stumbled on her heels. "Let us go. You don't know who you're messing with." She stared at Apollo with hope shining in her eyes.

Her trust stabbed into him. He had to do something. Apollo glared at Skinny, but not so much as a puff of smoke wafted above the man's head. Apollo growled.

George smirked and brandished his gun. "We know who you are Cassie. The secretary of state's daughter is a useful prize. I prefer to deliver you alive, but that's up to you."

The brick stalked toward Cassie with a rag clutched in his thick fingers.

She glanced to Apollo, panic stamped on her face, her mouth trembling.

He wouldn't allow abuse of his bride, no matter the cost to him. Apollo launched himself forward aiming for the brick, but two of the men lunged, slamming hard against him. Cassie screeched. Apollo's feet gave way. With his hands tied behind him, he couldn't stop his fall. His head thumped hard against the tile floor. The sound of bone cracking as a shock of pain spread over his skull. Sticky wetness dripped from his cheek. Blood smeared the floor. He tried to roll and right himself, but a boot pressed hard into his back pinning him. A new experience for him and he didn't care for it much.

George stood over him with the gun, Apollo dazed by pain. A meaty hand covered Apollo's mouth and nose with a damp cloth. He gulped a breath and all went black.

* * *

Apollo opened his eyes to slits. His face ached. He moved his jaw. Not broken, but his left cheek had swelled and a crust of rust-colored blood had formed over the gash, visible when he glanced down.

He was tied to a chair with Cassie secured to another. He didn't know where he was, but they had to escape. "Cassie," he whispered. She didn't move. Her head sagged forward and to the side. The length of her ebony hair hid her face. They must have been drugged.

Needing to devise a way out, Apollo surveyed the room. A few desks housing computers and other generic office furniture filled the space. Beige paint covered the walls and a large window showed the gray light of dusk. He couldn't see the street. From his view, muted green treetops swayed against deepening night. He guessed that they were about three floors up.

He strained at the ropes securing his wrists and numbing his fingers. The binding held. Irritation burned through his veins and he pulled with greater force. His skin was covered in beads of sweat. Nothing accomplished beyond his rising frustration and a damp shirt. He grumbled beneath his breath. Was this his end? He'd bested Hades by winning Cassie's love, but victory wasn't complete. Athens might yet be destroyed.

What a foul trick. His sister had warned him. Hades had to be at the root of this evil. No other creature held such disdain for humanity. If Apollo had access to his power, this spider's web would be wiped away with a thought and the spider with it. Apollo shook against the binding at his arms and feet, but the chair only trembled.

The click of a lock turning stopped his efforts. The door squeaked opened. John Medina strode in and closed the door. His head displayed an array of singed hair and burn marks. The grimace covering his mouth added to his ugly appearance. "You're awake." he said.

Apollo struggled.

Cassie lifted her head and blinked. She gasped. "John, what are you doing here? Quick, untie us."

Apollo sneered at Medina. "Cassie, John is one of them."

"No, he can't be."

Medina leaned his hip against a desk between Cassie and Apollo. "You're more intelligent than I thought, Goldilocks."

Apollo glared at Medina and focused his gaze with all his might. No flames or blue light ignited the rodent. Apollo yanked his arms, envisioning his hands around the mortal's neck. The ropes held.

Medina casually pulled a revolver from under his leather jacket and pointed it at Cassie's head. "Calm down, Goldilocks, or I'll have to do something to her."

Medina ambled next to Cassie and ran his vile hand across her cheek and down her neck. "We were interrupted last time." The weasel drooled. A glob hung in the corner of his mouth.

"Stop it." Cassie wrenched her face away to avoid Medina's touch. The insect chuckled.

Apollo's rage could ignite the room, if he were able. By Zeus, when he was free, he'd chain the man and hand him over to the Harpies for sport. Apollo ground out an oath. "You will die in the flames you planned for another."

The insect smirked. "If that's supposed to be a curse, you're wasting your breath I don't believe in them. You might as well relax. I have the hag and the boy. If you don't settle down, I can find all sorts of interesting ways to torture them."

"You monster," snapped Cassie.

"Oh, not me." He withdrew his hand from the swell of Cassie's breast. "That title belongs to our master."

"Hydra," growled Apollo.

"That's the brilliant mind behind everything," said Medina sneering at Apollo. "I'm amazed that you're smart enough to piece this together. Just for fun, tell me what you think is going to happen next?"

The rodent mocked them as if he were more than a scurvy little spider. Apollo had no patience for such disregard, but he had no choice but to bear it. A picture of Medina turned to stone entered his mind. If only he could immobilize with a glance. "Great Zeus. I will be eternally grateful for all of my gifts, if you will grant me this," he muttered under his breath.

Cassie trembled in her chair. "John. You don't

understand. People will die. We'll all die."

"You two will die. I'll be far away on a beach enjoying the pleasures of beautiful women."

"John. No." Tears glistened in her eyes.

Medina glanced at her. "Give it a rest."

The weasel strode back to Apollo. His dark eyes pits of evil. "I'd like to blow away that pretty face of yours." He pressed the cold gun barrel to Apollo's head. "Someone did nice work on your cheek. Wish I'd been there to finish the job, but I'll have my revenge. It turns out that Cassie won't be leaving here. You'll both take your chances with the bombs."

Cassie looked away. Apollo hardened his stare on the weasel. "The dignitaries have left. What good is the building?"

"Leveling the embassy will send a message, proving we can attack any target whenever and wherever we want. We have plans for those corrupt world leaders. One word from Hydra and the streets will run with blood."

Cassie's face blanched. "Have you no compassion or loyalty?"

"Only for himself," rumbled Apollo, the revolver still against his head.

"If you don't look out for number one, who will?" John pushed the barrel to Apollo's temple and his head swayed with the force.

"You're a freakin' sociopath," roared Cassie.

"A useful skill to Hydra." Medina turned his gaze to her. "No remorse, no hesitation to kill. You really shouldn't tempt a man like me. You'd both be dead now, but I have orders." He lowered the gun.

"And what about the old woman and the boy?" said Apollo, his temple throbbing.

"Jason? He's useful. The man who taught him decided he didn't want to blow up the train station. A silly moral objection about killing children and innocent people." Medina shook his head. "What an idiot. He'd already built the devices. After the man had a little accident, we picked up Jason." He grinned at Cassie and licked his lips. "I love my job."

"But not you. Nothing bothers you." Apollo spoke to distract John from Cassie.

"Not when it's in my interest. And Hydra pays very well."

Cassie shuddered. "There isn't enough money in all the world to murder people and betray your country."

Medina glared at her. "Sweet heart, that's easy to say when you've always had plenty of everything. I was dirt poor all my life until one of Hydra's cells recruited me. They accepted me, trained me. They value my unique talents. I'd hoped to infiltrate the FBI but your dad shut me down. You were my back-up plan until our date went bad. That's when Hydra ordered me to Athens."

"Disgusting excuse for a mortal," muttered Apollo. He'd scraped better camel dung from his sandal. "Do you think Hydra will let you live?"

Medina swung his arm back and hit Apollo in the face with his fist. His head jerked from the impact. The gash opened and swathed the rodent's knuckles with blood. Medina stared at the thick red smear on his hand and a sick smile twisted his mouth. "I'm important to them in ways you know nothing about. They value my loyalty. The current leaders demand power. Hydra will take it from them, and share it with us. I'm about to be a wealthy man."

Sobs tore from Cassie's throat.

"You go ahead and cry. Scream if you want, no one will help you," said Medina. "Our people are everywhere. You'd be surprised. In a few minutes, you'll be dead and Hydra will assume credit. The first of many displays of strength around the world."

Apollo despised being helpless and at the mercy of this insect. If he could get free for just a moment, he's squash the bug like a grape between his fingers.

Medina strutted toward the door. "I have an old woman to see before I catch my plane." The lock clicked behind him.

Cassie stared at Apollo with a combination of bewildered annoyance and rage. "Why don't you do something? You're a god, for hell's sake."

He winced. Apollo knew he'd have to tell her the truth some time, but he'd hoped for better circumstances. "I *was* a god."

* * *

Cassie felt her eyes bulge. She must have heard wrong. "What do you mean you *were* a god? Of course you're a god. You're Apollo. Zeus is your father." She knew she rambled, but couldn't stop the steady flow of words spewing from her lips. "You have a twisted sense of humor. Fry these damn bindings with your super laser vision. Do it and let's get out of here."

He shook his head. "I can't. Zeus punished me and made me mortal."

"That's ridiculous." A nervous laugh erupted from her. She hated this quirk. It only happened under extreme duress. "You're teasing me and it isn't funny." A series of snickers passed her lips. "Stop this sick joke and work your magic before I lose it." Cassie bit the inside of her cheek to keep from hysterics. She hoped he was kidding, because if he wasn't, they were in serious trouble.

"Look at me." He stared at her with a gaze as hard as marble and twice as cold. "I'm not teasing and I'm not telling a lie. I'm no longer a god and I have no power beyond that of other mortals."

"Damn it all to hell, you're serious," she said. Cassie wanted to scream, but knew it wouldn't do a bit of good. The truth sobered her. "When did this happen?" As soon as she'd voiced the question, she knew. Apollo had asked Zeus for help at her insistence. A pang of guilt stabbed her ribs. "You came back mortal?" she squeaked.

"Some help your father is. He's worse than Hydra. When were you going to tell me?"

"I'd hoped for an appropriate time." He shrugged. "The moment never came."

"Any time before now would have been good," she fumed, her long hair swaying around her with each agitated move of her head.

"There's no sense wasting time being angry. We need to think."

"There isn't time to think. Any moment, men with guns are going to shoot everyone before things start exploding."

The door creaked open. Cassie braced herself for John, but Jason's face appeared. "I heard you two were in here. You must have gone back to Andromeda's." He hurried in and pressed the door shut. Jason had bruises forming on his face and a swollen lip.

"How is Andromeda?" said Apollo. "Did they hurt her?"

Jason moved to untie him. "It was too much for her. I think she had a heart attack." He sniffed and wiped his nose on the sleeve of shirt. "She's dead."

Apollo's eyes rimmed red. His jaw hardened, and if he'd still been a god, Cassie was sure he'd level the place with his rage.

Jason finished freeing him and then moved on to Cassie's ropes. "They tie some mean knots," he said. "Andromeda told me to help you and get away. If I make it to America, I'm to give her brother's her love." A tear slid down his face, but he didn't bother to wipe it away.

Jason cleared his throat. "Let's go."

Cassie slipped out of the ropes, but Apollo hunkered in the chair. "You go. I need to stay and finish this."

"Are you kidding? We're about to be killed," said Cassie, pulling on Apollo's hands. "I've seen the massacre, remember?" She wanted to punch him herself. Maybe that hit to his head addled his brains. "We have to get out." She tugged on his arms. He didn't budge.

"We?" He looked at her, a golden brow riding high in question. "I'm going to see you both safe and then destroy these assassins. You're leaving."

Jason had set his chin in determination. "I can help. I owe it to Andromeda. There isn't time to dismantle the bombs, but we might get the people out before Hydra blows up the place."

"Aren't we guarded?" asked Cassie.

"Only a dozen men carrying guns. I heard them say the rest have gone," said Jason.

Apollo got to his feet. "Jason, do you know the guards locations? I need a distraction to get Cassie clear and the others out. Is that something you can manage?"

"That'll be easy," said Jason, grinning like a kid with a fat lip. "Most of them are in the dining room arguing over who's more important to Hydra and carving up positions for themselves in their new government."

"Did you happen to see a tall psycho with burns on his scalp?" Cassie asked. She'd like to get her hands on that creep.

"Oh, Medina? Yeah, he's arguing with the others. The only people outside are half a dozen guys patrolling the halls. They have guns, but they aren't much. I walked right by them. Sometimes looking younger pays."

"Do you have a few bombs available?" said Apollo.

"I know where I can get them."

"We'll need to barricade the doors of the dining room and set a trap before we escape."

Cassie glared at Apollo, her hands on her hips. "You're not getting rid of me this easy. I refuse to go without you. I'm sticking with you no matter what. Get use to it. How can I help?"

"And you thought you lacked courage." Apollo kissed her firmly on the mouth. "But I want you safe."

"Courage? Are you kidding?" Laughter bubbled up and she stuffed it down. "I'm about to wet my pants out of fear, but I'm more terrified of losing you than anything. We go together or not at all."

"Have it your way," Apollo grumbled. "But if there's a chance to flee, you take it."

She knew he wouldn't move until she agreed. "Fine." It was silly to fight. Cassie's dreams showed there wouldn't be time to escape.

CHAPTER TWENTY-ONE

Apollo sent Jason to scout out the hall before the three of them crept from the room. There was no one in sight, but that brought Apollo little comfort. Any moment an armed assassin might step into view. Mortal strength couldn't withstand bullets. He swallowed a growl. He needed a weapon or a miracle. The weapon would be easier to obtain.

The prophecy had showed Cassie cowering in a room. That much had changed and it proved the outcome might be altered. But to what end— something better or worse? He rolled his shoulders. He refused to think of defeat. He'd win the wager and they'd escape.

On stealthy feet, Apollo and Cassie carried the ropes that had restrained them, and headed to the closed double doors of the dining room where raised voices argued. Apollo slipped the ropes through the door handles and tied them fast. It wouldn't hold them long.

Cassie seemed to read his thoughts. She gestured toward a large chest beside the doors.

"How about this?" she whispered.

Apollo glanced to the heavy furniture and shook his head. He'd have to drag it over the floor. "Noise," he mouthed to her. They'd need a loud distraction to cover the scraping sound. So far, Jason hadn't created a distraction of any kind and he'd been gone too long. Where was he?

Shots rang out.

The sound reverberated through the hall and he and Cassie scurried on their bellies, Apollo shielding her with his body. He hoped this was Jason's distraction and that the boy was all right. Heavy shoes pounded and the dining room doors rattled as those inside yanked on the handles to get out. Apollo got to his feet and shoved the chest against the straining portal, the screech of wood against wood muffled by shouts. "That will have to do," he said, breathing heavily from the exertion.

Cassie lifted her head, jumped up and joined Apollo with her back against the wall beside the doors.

"Where's Jason?" Apollo murmured. Each moment pricked at his nerves for the boy's safety.

Cassie's legs shook, but she made no sound and leaned around the corner to view an adjoining hall. She snapped back flat against the wall. "Jason's coming."

The boy hurried toward them lugging a canvas sack. Fear in his wide eyes and his urgent actions suggested they had little time.

"What's this?" said Apollo.

Jogging to the chest, Jason put down the sack and frantically yanked out what appeared to be a bomb. "What it looks like," said Jason. "Why just make it look like it would blow up, when I can make it explode for real?" Jason set to work as Apollo and Cassie kept watch.

Fists pounded the doors and then something large slammed against the inside.

"Where are the guards?" Apollo asked.

"Downstairs," said Jason focused on his work. "They're putting out a fire."

"Fire?" whispered Apollo. "Is the embassy going to burn down around us?"

Cassie shook her head. "No, the automatic sprinkler system will put it out."

"Nope," said Jason, glancing at her for a moment and then returning to his task. "I dismantled it. There's a utility room with all kinds of controls and wiring. It was locked, but I'm almost as good at breaking into places as I am at blowing things up." Jason's fingers flew over multi-colored wires.

The boy was a marvel, but the sound of boots thudded toward them. "How much longer?" said Apollo, sweat trickling down his neck. Adrenaline coursed through his limbs in preparation for battle.

The vibration of hard heels on wood came nearer.

"Almost done," breathed Jason. He snatched

the device and wedged his body behind the chest out of view.

Another loud bang and the doors quivered.

John Medina stalked toward them, his revolver trained on Apollo. Air sucked out of his lungs. This was not an improvement on the dream.

"Drop to your knees," the rodent growled.

Apollo stood his ground. No insect would order him to grovel.

Medina shifted and leveled his weapon on Cassie. "Both of you."

Cassie lowered to her knees with a defiant glare.

How dare this gnat. Given the chance, Apollo would snap his neck. "By the gods and great Zeus, I'll kill you."

"By the gods?" Medina laughed. "No one believes in gods. No one with half a brain, that is. What are you going to tell me next, Goldilocks? That Zeus is your daddy and he'll strike me dead? If gods existed, there wouldn't be a need for Hydra."

Apollo grumbled under his breath a combination curse on the man and plea to Zeus. He wouldn't count on divine intervention, but it didn't hurt to ask. Apollo knelt beside Cassie. The act of obedience he only gave to his father caused his blood to boil.

Medina moved closer. Perspiration covered his brow and he shifted on his feet, glancing this way and that. The man feared. If Apollo surprised him at the right moment, he could take him down.

John nodded to the chest barring the doors. "Your handiwork? Move it."

A thud struck the doors. Wood cracked. Apollo couldn't allow Jason to be exposed. This vile creature would kill him on sight.

Cassie trembled beside him. "You're an idiot, John." She choked and then sniggered. "The whole place is about to explode." Laughter won out and she giggled.

Apollo knew she couldn't help the fit brought on by terror, but the dark glare in Medina's eyes warned violence.

"Don't laugh at me," Medina ground through clenched teeth. He stood over her, a demon deciding on his form of torment.

Cassie pressed her lips tight, but hysterics burst through. "Sorry," she giggled.

"Stop it," Medina yelled and launched a ruthless kick to her gut. Cassie flew back and sprawled against the floor, gasping. The insect glared at her. "That'll stop you, bitch."

Shock and rage ignited Apollo's fury. He flung himself at Medina, struggling for control of the gun. He wrenched the rodent's wrist to free the weapon.

Medina clutched the gun tighter and bit down on Apollo's arm, growling like a rabid hound. Blood ran from the wound, red drops pelting the floor. Apollo refused to let go and twisted harder.

Medina gasped and stopped biting. Apollo punched him. Medina grabbed Apollo by the front of his shirt as he fell, pulling Apollo to the ground with him.

Medina pressed the gun to Apollo's gut. An evil grin spread over his mouth. "This will hurt like hell."

Apollo grabbed for the gun and they rolled across the floor.

The gun fired.

Apollo watched Cassie's mouth open as if to scream, but heard nothing. He staggered to his feet.

Blood spread under Medina in a widening puddle. He lifted the gun with shaky hands, gasping, his mouth moving like a fish out of water struggling to breathe. Ruby fluid bubbled from the wound in his neck. The gun slipped from his fingers, hitting the floor with a dull thud. Medina convulsed and let out a gurgle through his throat. His eyes fixed.

Apollo retrieved the gun. He owed his life to this mortal invention. Perhaps other contraptions held worth. He'd rethink his views on human science, once they escaped.

Cassie pulled herself up, rubbing her ribs.

Jason had crawled out from behind the chest. "Fifteen minutes and Hydra's bombs ignite."

"We need more time," said Cassie. "There's no way we can get everyone out."

The doors buckled as those inside pushed to

escape.

Jason scrunched his mouth. "Most people are locked in a room downstairs, but some might be hiding."

"You two get out, I'll see to the rest," said Apollo.

Cassie shook her head. "Together or not at all."

Jason stared at his watch. "Ten minutes left."

"Have it your way," Apollo grumbled. "No time to argue, we have to move."

They fled the corridor, down the stairs and through the second floor. A door on the right vibrated with pounding and screams for help.

"This is the room," said Jason. "Seven minutes."

"You go ahead and I'll meet you outside," said Apollo, moisture trickling down his back.

Cassie hesitated. "No. I can't."

"Go. I'll be all right." Apollo nudged her forward. "Zeus won't let me die." He wished that were true.

"Six minutes."

"You be outside in four minutes." Cassie's chin trembled. "I love you." She kissed him before Jason yanked her arm and dragged her downstairs.

Apollo slammed into the door with his shoulder. It shuddered under his attack, but didn't open. "Stand back," he yelled to those inside. Apollo pulled a long table from the wall, lined the end up with the opening and shoved with all his might, using it as a battering ram. The door splintered and burst open. Terrified people escaped through the opening, panic on their faces as they passed him.

Apollo latched on to a young woman. "Is there anyone else?"

She stared wild-eyed. "I don't know, let me go." She ripped her arm from him and ran with the rest of the frightened rabbits.

Apollo opened doors and made a desperate search on his way to the main level, and safety. People raced past him down the stairs.

An explosion rumbled and rocked the building.

Beams and debris crashed around him. Chunks of plaster fell, leaving a fine white powder. Shrieks echoed and smoke poured in. Apollo tore through the structure.

Another blast.

Blue flames danced above his head, licking the exposed beams. Sooty smoke hung chest high. The acrid smell filled his nose and burned his lungs. Apollo coughed and dropped to the floor. He sucked in air and crawled forward feeling his way.

Cassie and Jason had to be safe. "Please, almighty Zeus, grant me that," he breathed.

Fire spread down the walls. In a few moments the building would go up like a torch. Apollo squinted through deadly haze. His eyes burned and streamed from irritation. Stifling heat covered him with sweat. He swallowed the bitter taste of ash as he gulped a breath close to the floor.

A cough hacked in the next room.

Apollo hugged the ground and listened. He willed his body to move through heat scorching his lungs in the direction of the sound.

Another cough.

A body huddled on the ground. Apollo coughed and latched on to the older man. His face smudged black and his hands burned, but he was alive. Apollo dragged his thin body into the hall.

The building crackled with heat like Hades' furnace. Each breath a struggle. Heaving the man onto his back, Apollo crawled with his burden toward escape.

Another blast.

The widows exploded.

CHAPTER TWENTY-TWO

"He'll make it. He has to," said Jason at her side.

Cassie watched from outside as fire engulfed the building. The structure shuddered. Part of the roof collapsed with a roar and a wave of white heat. Her throat clogged with tears. She fixated on the inferno. Flames threatened the trees, their orange tails leaping thirty feet. She must have been in shock. People moved in slow motion. Smoke belched into the night sky. The acrid smell burned her nose.

"No chance of survival," said the fireman.

She couldn't look away. Horror and disbelief kept her focused on carnage. "No chance of survival," she murmured. The world swirled around her. Voices jumbled into a low hum. Embers floated like gray snow and then everything faded out.

* * *

Cassie sat in a hospital room. Light shone through the window and filled the room. She'd collapsed at the scene. Her parents had admitted her for observation after her constant rant about marrying a Greek god and needing to find him. Then followed her three days of silence. She lifted her hand and tenderly caressed the gold band on her finger. A tear slid down the side of her nose.

Days after the attack when the ashes had cooled, bones of one grown male were found a few feet from the door. Another was extracted from the ruble, burned beyond recognition. Due to the explosive force, a number of body parts scattered the area, making identification a gruesome and painstaking task. She couldn't even bury him.

The media applauded Cassie and Jason for saving fifteen people, but Apollo deserved the credit. She swallowed hard as each painful thought cut through her like a razor. This wound would never heal.

Cassie's parents were bursting with pride. Her mother had made Jason her pet project, and arranged for his travel, his lodging and education in the US. At least some good had come of all the misery.

Fifteen people were saved, but not the man she loved. Cassie pressed her face into her pillow. Her shoulders shook. Silent as a knife, grief wracked her body and sliced her heart.

CHAPTER TWENTY-THREE

I must be dead.

Light surrounded Apollo. His singed clothing traded for a white toga appropriate for his judgment before Zeus and the gods. He rubbed his hand over his bald head, his golden mane gone, melted in the scorching inferno. It didn't matter. Nothing did without Cassie.

Hades would collect on their wager. To serve that walking corpse in the land of smoldering brimstone brought back the agony of his last moments. Apollo shivered. He could still smell smoke and taste ash on his tongue. And Cassie...his heart broke for Cassie.

Apollo stood in the court of the gods. Hades licked his thin, chalky lips in anticipation of his prize. Muffling a growl, Apollo turned to his father.

Zeus wore a deep red robe and stared at him, stern as ever. "I have something to say to my son." His father rose from his golden throne, his arms outstretched to the gods and goddesses that would hear Apollo's fate.

Apollo knelt, bowing his naked head before Zeus, and awaited the chains he'd be forced to wear as Hades' slave.

"You've done well," said Zeus.

Apollo jerked his head up. His father smiled at him and then turned toward Hades. "You have lost our wager. My son saved lives and gained Cassandra's love."

Hades snarled. "The bet between Apollo and myself was that he would save the embassy. He failed in that."

Zeus shook his silver head at Hades. "The embassy is not only a building, but also the ambassador and his people. Apollo saved most of them. My son is the victor. I have spoken."

Apollo couldn't fathom what happened. He was dead, but not in servitude to his uncle. A great mercy from his father.

Hades' mouth twisted. "You cheat me, brother," he muttered upon his bronze throne and shook his bony fist at Zeus.

Zeus waved him off. "Stop your cursing and don't touch Apollo or Cassandra in a vengeful tantrum."

Apollo couldn't believe it.

Zeus grinned and a spark of sea-green and blue lit his eyes. "Hades and I had a small side bet. If you gained Cassandra's love and saved the embassy as a mortal, then you'd win and I'd gain Hades' service."

Apollo thought to point out that the original

wager was that Hades would serve Apollo, but he thought better than to bring up any petty grievance. Besides, Zeus would prove a much harder taskmaster. Cassie would live her life, as she should have three thousand years ago. Apollo swallowed the lump in his throat. *Without me.* A fair trade, his life lost so Cassie might live hers. Gratitude welled up inside. He bowed to his father. "Thank you. I am forever in your debt."

Zeus chuckled. "You have earned my favor. I return your full rights as a son of Zeus, a god, bringer of light, prophecy, music and all the other gifts you possessed before your wager with Hades, including your golden mane."

"I'm not dead?" Instantly his scalp was covered in thick blond waves that brushed his shoulders.

"How could such a valiant son be left to dwindle in the underworld?" His father's gaze dimmed and his brow furrowed. "Cassandra is suffering over your loss. It's time you went to her."

* * *

Cassie dressed in black and stood beside the olive tree where they'd made vows to each other. Tears clouded her vision, but she didn't need to see clearly. The spot was etched into her memory. She rubbed her tired eyes. Apollo visited her in dreams, a blessing and a curse. When she dreamed she felt him, tasted his lips and breathed in his honeyed scent.

But when she woke…. her mouth quivered. The loss of him hit her all over again.

She sniffed and spoke to Apollo as if he were with her. "Sometimes I think I'll die from missing you."

A flash of light.

Cassie squinted and shielded her eyes with her hand. Apollo's golden form stood before her. She lowered her gaze to the ground. "When am I going to stop imagining you?"

The vision reached for her, pulled her into his arms and took her mouth with passion. She melted against him. He couldn't be real, but at the moment she didn't care.

Apollo released her mouth. "I am real," he breathed against her lips.

"But you can't be." She shook her head to chase away the illusion.

"Touch me."

Cassie blinked and stretched out her fingers to his face, caressing his skin, the hard planes and valleys, then his shoulders and his white toga edged in gold. She trembled. "But you were mortal. You died. How?"

"Zeus rewarded me. I'm again Apollo, god of prophecy…and your husband."

She stared at him. Desperate for it to be true and fearing it was a delusion. "I can't believe it."

"Must I convince you each time of my existence?"

Those same words he'd said to her in a classroom weeks before shook her. "It's you. It's really you." She wiped her stinging eyes. "You know, when most people die, they don't come back."

"I'm not most people." He stroked the side of her face with the tips of his fingers, leaving a trail of warmth.

Cassie pressed her cheek into his palm. "No, you're not."

It had been weeks since the attack. She'd been crying her eyes out thinking she'd lost him forever. Cassie lifted her head and pinned him with her gaze. "Where the hell were you? Gallivanting around Olympus?" She stabbed his chest with her finger. "You're a god who thinks he's a freakin' hero. No more of that. I can't take you dying on me again."

"Beloved," he whispered as he held her. "You won't have to. We'll live a long life, have children, and spend eternity together."

She stared at him through blurriness. "Children? But what about Hydra? That maniac is still out there."

"Don't worry." Apollo kissed along her hairline. "Zeus is sending Hermes to deal with him."

THE END

Thank you
For purchasing APOLLO'S GIFT.

Watch for the second book in the Greek Gods Series.
Available in the winter of 2014.

BETRAYED

Trust is required for betrayal to flourish.
Betrayal has made Bram a swaggering vampire with something to prove. Unfortunately, his opportunity for vindication arises when his brother is kidnapped by Bram's enemy and held in Rome's catacombs. If Bram fails to free him, his brother will suffer torture and die. Bram would never forgive himself. His only chance of success may be a human.

Beautiful Angela Russo, has polish, connections, and a grudge. The vampires have stripped her family of power and position, destroying their lives. Forgiveness isn't one of Angela's virtues. She is used to getting what she wants, and what Angela wants is revenge.

When Bram and Angela are forced into a reluctant alliance, the secrets they uncover shatter everything they have believed to be true.

Can they learn to forgive the past and work together before blood runs in the streets?

Available in the summer of 2013.

Enjoy the following excerpt
from the Kivronian Vampire Series.

CONQUERED

CHAPTER ONE

Earth
Twenty-years in the future.

It shouldn't happen like this. A man has a right to his dignity. Rafe Nucretah narrowed his sharp eyes in the moonless autumn night and surveyed the damage. Utah's southern desert stretched before him, parched red dirt and wild sage littered with massacred flesh. He strode toward a rumpled mass on the sandy ground. His jaw clenched as he stared into the tender face of a murdered child, five years old maybe, round cheeked with golden curls. Human. Her sweet visage reminded him of his sister. He swallowed and turned away.

"Dante," Rafe croaked, then coughed to clear what lodged in his throat. "How many?"

His younger brother stood tall and slender, dressed in the jet-black uniform of an Enforcer. Dante's dark eyes flashed with rage "Eighteen. Three are my men, the rest human."

Rafe shook his head against the loss. *How could this happen?*

"Were there signs of the madness?" Dante's dark gaze narrowed hard as obsidian.

"None that I detected last week." Rafe's stomach knotted. Surely some nervous laughter and rambling didn't mean anything. *My recent fatigue is nothing. I'm not at risk. Not yet.* "Where is Hebric?"

Dante moved closer, silent. "Skulking around The Devil's Garden. Follow the trail of blood with caution. I know he's your friend, but I doubt he'll recall that fact before he tries to fry you with his Nova sword."

Friend. When the *Rosh* madness hit, there were no friends, but Rafe owed Hebric his life. Frustration grew in him, rising like a demon. Too late to save his childhood friend, the best he could manage was a dignified end, a warrior's death in battle.

Rafe swore to himself in the ancient language. This shouldn't happen. Hebric was close to a thousand-years-old, but he should've had fifty years before the madness hit. *I should have that much.*

Pressure crushed Rafe's chest. The thought of killing the man he loved as a brother brought the bitter taste of bile into his mouth, combining with the reality before him. If Rafe failed, Hebric would have his name and deeds expunged from the annals, as if he'd never existed: the worst fate possible.

Rafe clenched his fists. *I will not fail.* Hebric must die with his weapon in hand to maintain his place of honor and continue in the other realms. Rafe determined he'd give him that chance.

Rafe lifted his nose to the air. The coppery smell of blood mingled with death to fill his senses, familiar and unwelcome. For a moment, Rafe's thoughts lay chained on another world. His heart pounded and he shook himself violently back to Earth. He breathed through the wrenching memory.

"I have the Enforcers cleaning up this mess. Bram won't arrive for another week," said Dante. "If the media gets a hold of it this time, there will be real trouble."

"Trouble? A tame word for insurrection. If the rebels hear of it, I doubt if even Talon can dissuade revolt. Our existence depends on maintaining control." Rafe felt the weight of decision and rolled his shoulders. If humans learned the truth, they'd fight, and every drop of their blood was precious. "Don't worry. I'll post the dead as having transferred to Kivron, as usual. I can handle the heat from the High Council." Rafe clenched his teeth. He hated the politics, the lies, and the senseless end of life.

Rafe pulled his Neutron Eliminator from the loop on his belt and followed the carnage across the sun-baked ground. His black leather boots crunched against sand over stone until he stopped at the next rise, grateful his battle suit hid him in the darkness.   Even crazed, Hebric would be difficult to overcome. "This way." He beckoned Dante and the Enforcers to back him up, and pushed down the despair threatening his focus.

The trailhead loomed ahead, towering rock walls with scrub oak eerily gray in the night. The cool desert wind rustled his hair and Rafe brushed it back from his wary eyes. His claws lengthened in preparation. Rafe knew the vampire's talents and steeled himself against what might lie ahead, waiting for him in the shadows.

The Enforcers positioned themselves around the sandstone pillars with their jagged outcroppings. Rafe took a few steps in the direction of the sizzle from a Nova sword and the stink of burning flesh. "Hebric, come out and let's talk." Concern thickened Rafe's tone as he stalked nearer.

"No. I'm busy," rasped a voice ahead and to Rafe's right.

Rafe's fangs lengthened. "Too busy for an old friend? It's Rafe Nucretah. We were in school together and fought side by side in the war on Kivron. You remember?" He crept forward.

"Rafe?"

"Yes." He skulked around a twisted cedar, the

woodsy scent masking his own. "I've come to visit." Feelings of sorrow, love, and pity warred within him. He had to remain sharp and tamp down the uncomfortable emotions.

Another sizzle from the Nova sword. "Are you hungry? Join me for a meal." Hebric's voice thinned on the breeze.

The stench of charred flesh wafted toward Rafe. He cringed, fearing what he'd find. "Don't go to any trouble on my behalf. We can talk about the time you saved my life. You were the bravest of all." Rafe slipped through the rock passage.

"I remember. It's no trouble. I just sliced off a juicy limb. Join me."

"*Silch.*" Rafe sprinted past a boulder, tore through the passage, and halted before a cleft in the rock. He peered in.

There, with his back against the rough sandstone sat Hebric, his large powerful build wearing his charcoal dress uniform. His fangs dripped red as he held up his own severed leg. "It's fresh," he wheezed.

Rafe wanted to turn away from the morbid sight, but couldn't. How could he bring his friend to a respectful end if he couldn't fight? The madness had brought a valiant warrior to this, and it tore at Rafe's heart. His comrade and trusted friend, lost to him. He fought back the tears stinging behind his eyes as he cautiously stepped closer. Bile rose and Rafe swallowed it, willing his mouth to smile. "I see that."

He moved beside his friend, picked up the sword lying in the dirt, and held it out to Hebric. He ignored it and continued to stare at the flesh in his hands. Rafe swallowed hard, accepted the juicy limb from his friend, and then pressed the weapon into Hebric's palm.

"Fight me." Rafe waved his own weapon above Hebric's head.

"You want games? I'm tired, Rafe. Perhaps I've eaten too much. After a nap." Hebric's head bobbed and his eyelids lowered to slits.

"No! Take a swipe at me." Rafe taunted him, desperate to get him to act.

"Later. Aren't you hungry? " Hebric's gray eyes opened briefly.

Dante and the rest circled around Rafe, disgust and grim acceptance stamped on their faces. Hebric grimaced, and his pale brows furrowed. "You brought company. I don't believe one leg will be enough." He dropped the Nova sword and his arm fell at his side.

Rafe's throat closed as he hunkered down beside his friend. Hebric was dead. Grief twisted his gut. "I'm sorry, old friend. I've failed you," he murmured. "I've eternally failed you."

The crimson flood coated the dirt and soles of Rafe's black boots, making them slide against the rock as he turned toward Dante.

"He wasn't yet one thousand," said Dante, his skin paler than usual.

"No."

Dante set his shadowed gaze on Rafe. "He waited too long."

"We all know the risk of nearing a thousand years. Hebric thought he had time." Rafe schooled his emotions and watched understanding burden his brother's face.

"He was two years younger than you," whispered Dante.

"Are you worried for my sanity? Don't be. I'm not Hebric. I'll be safe after I claim a mate." Rafe rubbed the back of his neck. "Hebric admitted to being too choosy."

"But no unattached male is safe from the madness once he reaches one thousand, not even you."

Rafe winced inwardly. "I'm well aware of my situation." He looked on Hebric's mangled body. "I'll take care of it."

# # #

Three nights since the carnage in the desert and Rafe still couldn't shake the vile images from his mind. He'd done all in his power to save Hebric's honor and had failed. The memory of Kivronian blood still lay heavy in his nose. When he'd returned home that night, he'd had his battle suit and blood stained boots destroyed. He couldn't look on them without seeing his own destruction.

The signs of madness were becoming impossible to ignore, clouded thinking, occasional confusion, and the slight impairment of his natural abilities were only the beginning. So far, he'd kept his illness hidden. But how long could his gift for logic withstand the insanity that had shredded Hebric's mind? *I must act tonight.*

He dressed in a charcoal suit, shirt, and crimson tie. Red was the sacred color for loss. Now, his tie was the only respect he could allow without drawing attention. Through three nights of mourning in secret, Rafe had worn the red robe in his rooms as he burned all correspondence and memorabilia from his friend. Hebric's multiple offences, succumbing to madness, slaughtering humans, the source of Kivronian life, and then to die as he did—disgraced without redemption, made it an offense to whisper his name. As of dawn today, Hebric never existed. Tears welled up, but Rafe fought the display. *Enough.* Silent memories were all he had left of the man he'd loved as a brother.

Tonight, he'd act before he fell to the same fate. Rafe's heart wasn't in the search for a mate, but he refused to let Hebric's death count for nothing. *I'll do my duty in your honor—and live.*

Rafe found Dante in the dining room, sipping a glass of blood from a crystal goblet. Normally, Rafe enjoyed the conversations shared in this room of dark wood and yellow walls, but not on this night. Taking a deep breath, Rafe broached the uncomfortable subject. "It's been scheduled. I'll secure a mate tonight."

Dante sat back in the heavy oak chair and studied his brother. "You've decided on a human female, then. Who is she? The South American Ambassador's daughter or the attaché from China?"

After the ache of Hebric's loss, Rafe understood his brother's concern for him, but it didn't ease his task. "There are plenty of attractive females on Earth. For once, my position as

Governor isn't important, survival is. I won't take months to woo an appropriate prize. I should've taken care of this before now. I knew my time was drawing short. I just...."

Hebric's blood, darkening the sand invaded Rafe's mind and he shook his head against it. "I'll make a claim."

"Do you have one in mind?"

"No, but since waiting to win one of our own females in the lottery isn't an option I can afford, I'll make due with a human." Rafe felt desperation churning his insides. He couldn't chance putting it off, couldn't meet the same end as his comrade. Another violent twist of his heart made Rafe rub his stinging eyes with his fingers. "I'll have a bride."

Dante's jet-black brows traveled up. "You can't mean to bind yourself to a female you barely know. I realize the situation has been difficult and the loss, great, but this is for eternity. Couldn't you wait until our brother and sire return?"

"Don't worry, Bram will understand and our

sire will be relieved it's done. I'm taking precautions. The women will be fully vetted by Match Maker Registry. Many females seek Kivronian husbands and will accept if I offer. It's been done by others." Rafe leaned forward and locked eyes with Dante. "Better to be bound to a stranger and live, than face insanity and be expunged from the annals. I mean to survive."

Within the hour, Rafe sped down the darkened highway through the desert, lit only by the stars, and the headlights of his black Bentley. The Kivronian vehicles he owned were faster, but he enjoyed the vintage car. Control rested solely in his hands, rather than the voice-activated computer. *Hebric hates this car. Hated.*

His friend's death sliced through him like a Nova sword. Rafe grimaced, pressed harder on the accelerator and flew past the cremation facility. His comrade's torso had turned to ash within hours. The remnants scattered to the winds while his head had sat prominently displayed to ridicule for three nights. Even his skull had been ground to dust by now. Hebric had been valiant, a warrior of the first order. He deserved better.

Rafe pulled himself from the painful thoughts and focused on the task at hand. Claiming a mate should be a joyful undertaking, but not under the present circumstances. The binding would stunt madness, but not cure it. Only his mate's love would hold such power. Even if she did grow to love him enough, the binding would end his chance of having children. Humans couldn't bear their young. It's the reason Hebric had put off taking a mate, hoping to win a Kivronian female in the 1ottery. They'd spoken of it often since invading Earth. The joy of little ones, teaching them to fight, making sure they grew into valiant warriors, true, brave, and strong. It's also the reason Rafe had procrastinated. *That future is gone.* His fingers tightened on the wheel.

The goal of claiming a female would have to coincide with business. He had a sector to run, and the nasty business of covering up the massacre of eighteen people. A statement had been sent to the media the next day. The immediate transfer of humans to his home planet rarely occurred, most often when an accidental loss of life made it a necessary ploy. He hoped the rebels believed it. His jaw tightened. Only a direct order from the High Council could make him engage in such deceit. Duty and survival of his people made his compliance imperative. But he didn't like it.

At least, the issue of claiming a mate would be done by evening's end. His assistant had scheduled a parade of eligible young women for Rafe to peruse between meetings. *Ridiculous. What kind of person would degrade herself in that way?* He couldn't imagine, and didn't relish finding out. "Some social climber or a girl desperate to further her career," he grumbled.

Rafe scowled. The tires screeched and threw

red sand as he took the turn into town. He'd known one day he'd likely have to claim a human. There were few Kivronian females left after the civil war, but the High Council claimed most and dangled the rest before their males in the lottery. Chances of winning against such odds were miniscule.

Humans were illogical, fragile, and their culture confusing. And now he must bind himself to such a creature? Rafe chafed at the idea. He demanded order. Lived and breathed the neat, controlled existence of the military. No matter the difficulties, he'd make it work. *I'm in control of the situation.*

Rafe halted before the government complex and killed the engine. He would accomplish his objective, find a female who wasn't overly annoying, claim and bind her. With his superior senses and intellect, he should be able to pick a suitable mate, even in Red Rock, Utah.

# # #

Pepper sat poised in Governor Nucretah's waiting area, her laptop computer balanced on her skirt-clad thighs as she typed notes for her latest assignment. Landing an interview with Governor Rafe Nucretah was a coup. She'd been trying for months. Though he'd agreed, she'd shown up every night for the last three, sitting in the hall, trying to get in to see the most powerful, and reportedly, devastatingly handsome, alien vampire in the Western Quadrant. Tonight he was available, and Pepper had finally been allowed past the front desk. She refused to leave without seeing him.

Months ago, Pepper had graduated from writing the food section of the *Red Rock Times* to fulfill her dream job: investigative reporter. She'd longed to sink her teeth into reporting on political corruption and to tear it wide open. The public had a right to know. Even though, after the alien take-over there wasn't much a human could do to change things. Still, knowledge was power. Humanity needed information, and Pepper Morgan was just the girl to give it to them.

This assignment was nothing special. Yet another group of humans had been transferred to the planet, Kivron. The real story was the man who authorized the transfers. That's what she'd told her editor, but Pepper had begged for the assignment for other reasons than a story.

Worry over her father kept her up at night. Her concern had grown until it had possessed her thoughts and had railed at her every waking moment. Information didn't cause her anxiety, but the lack of it. Pepper trusted her gut. She hadn't heard from her father, except for the few letters that came by way of the inter-galactic transporter, and they were infrequent. *So unlike him. Something is very wrong.*

Six months ago, he'd been transferred. "Shanghaied, was more like it," she muttered to herself. She'd returned home from work to find an official letter on the kitchen table next to her father's blue coffee cup. *The services of Dr. Ben Morgan were required for an indefinite interval.* His clothes and essentials were gone, but he'd left the sweater she'd made him last Christmas. Little things like that gnawed at her. His favorite ratty sneakers cluttered the floor of his closet. Those things she could attribute to the speed of his leaving, but not the photo of her mom. He always kept it next to his bed. He'd have taken that—if he could have.

Her father was a renowned biologist and useful to the aliens. She was proud of him. His search for a cure for the ruthless plague that had devastated Earth's population had taken most of his time. He would have forgotten to eat, if she hadn't shoved a plate of food under his nose. He would tease her about her cooking. The toast was too brown and the eggs were too wet. She blinked back moisture and wiped her cheek. He'd eat every crumb.

Her mother had succumbed to the disease at its height, ten years ago. Civilization had dissolved into chaos as the body count had mounted. Pepper shuddered. Fearful thoughts of those days haunted her. Earth had become a war zone. Her stomach knotted. She'd been fifteen. There were no words dark enough to capture those months of loss and devastation.

And then the aliens came.

Kivronian medicine had proved their salvation. Working with her father, the deaths ended and society reordered. Humanity owed its life to the vampires—and the invaders meant to collect. She closed her laptop and fisted her hands in her lap. *At least when Mom died, I had the chance to say, "Goodbye".*

A gaggle of young women fluttered into the waiting area, all well dressed and dripping sophistication.

"Ladies, I'm Celeste, Mr. Nucretah's assistant. Make sure we have your current information so we can contact you."

Pepper studied the slight, coal haired vampire. She had the most unusual silver eyes. Her blood red lips, set against bone white flesh, might have been appealing, if she didn't make Pepper's skin crawl. *Call it intuition or a hunch, but there's something creepy about that woman.* After three nights, Pepper thought she'd seen everyone, but not Celeste. Apparently, if Nucretah didn't show up, neither did his assistant. *Rough life.*

Turning her focus to the women, Pepper could see that any one of them could have been a model or a beauty queen, if those industries had still existed. Who were they? Too refined for hookers, and too well dressed to need a job, these women looked like exotic jewels, born to adorn a powerful man's arm.

Pepper ran her hand over her navy wool skirt. The suit was well made, and still in decent shape for being second hand, but her white blouse was almost new. She pulled a loose thread from her jacket and sat up a little straighter.

Watching the group with rapt attention, Pepper continued her speculation. They wore make-up and jewelry. A few bothered to style their hair in a sleek Kivronian knot, a sort of French twist that bared their necks. Alluring to vampires.

Most humans couldn't afford cosmetics and Pepper went about fresh-faced. Her dad used to say her skin didn't need help and her cheeks were blessed with a natural rosy glow. *Oh Dad, how I miss you*. One of the beauties wore false lashes. Bambi would kill to have eyes like those. Pepper sighed. *Who am I kidding*? Her clump of auburn hair was too thick and hung to her waist. Her eyes weren't anything spectacular. She should be grateful she wasn't competing with those goddesses. What were they doing here?

Being the investigative reporter she was, Pepper marched up to the girl with the lashes, who wore a cream silk dress, and began interrogating. "Lovely dress. Is this for a photo shoot?" Pepper waved her arm to include the clan of beauties.

Miss Silk looked Pepper up and down like she was a poor cut of meat. "So you're not one of us. I didn't think so."

Pepper wanted to kick Miss Silk in the shin, but smiled. "I'm here to do a story. I'm a reporter."

"Oh!" The woman turned toward the clucking mob. "Girls, they've sent a reporter. They're doing a story about us."

The women hovered around Pepper like kids promised free candy, all talking at once.

"Excuse me, one at a time," Pepper shouted above the din of excited females. Being near six feet in height, she garnered their attention and addressed herself to Miss Silk. "Can you tell me what brought you here tonight?"

As Miss Silk opened her mouth to answer, Mr. Nucretah's assistant clapped her bony hands. "Quiet, ladies. The Governor is ready to see you. And remember, only speak when asked."

Pepper's gaze flew to the model-skinny assistant. Raising her hand over the heads of the eager crowd, Pepper caught her attention. "They're getting in to see Mr. Nucretah?"

"Yes, yes. You all are. Line up and enter in an orderly fashion." The assistant moved to the office door. "He'll look you over and make his decision. Once he's voiced his preference, it's final. Those not chosen will leave quickly and quietly."

After waiting three nights in a stiff metal chair, Pepper wasn't about to miss her chance. She fell in line behind Miss Silk. Whatever they were vying for, Pepper intended to stick around long enough to ask Nucretah some questions. *I have to get to my dad and the Governor is the only man who can help. Nothing matters more. To hell with the story.*

The assistant herded them into the plush office. A hush fell on the group as they took in the splendor of thick Persian carpet, black leather chairs, and a sleek onyx desk where the most captivating man Pepper had ever seen, held court.

Rafe Nucretah scanned the line up and Pepper's mouth went dry. He was up to something. She felt it in her gut and she always trusted her intuition. Any man who looked that gorgeous had to be guilty of some crime. Being an alien vampire and a politician increased the likelihood.

He rose from his desk with the fluid grace of a predator and stalked toward them. His chiseled features, sleek black hair, and dark brown eyes made it difficult to think. *Get a grip, girl*. He was only the most attractive man she'd ever seen, but her father's situation may be serious and she had to keep her head.

When his gaze rested on her, heat filled her cheeks and trickled down to her belly. She had to keep her wits. *Like me. Like me.* She ran the mantra through her mind and flashed her most charming smile. He raised an ebony brow, but showed no other interest.

"Turn, please," said the assistant.

They each made a slow rotation. It reminded Pepper of the, now-defunct, Westminster Dog Show. And she doubted she'd win "best of breed". *How humiliating*.

Once the line had completed its turn and

again faced the Greek god, Pepper knew what he'd say a nanosecond before the words escaped his full lips.

"This one." He nodded at Pepper.

She jerked her head to stare at the man who'd chosen her over all the lovelies. Maybe he needed a secretary or some menial laborer. No chance he'd picked her over the ravishing girls to be an accessory at a state dinner. It didn't matter. She'd do anything if he'd help her father.

"The rest of you will now leave." The assistant held the door open. "The front desk will validate for parking."

Miss Silk sneered at Pepper as she glared through her lashes and flounced out with the rest of the grumbling pack. At this point, Pepper braced herself to lay her case at his feet. *I'll kiss his feet if it'll help*. The moist fingers of her left hand tightened on her computer, snugly tucked under her arm. Sweat dampened her skin wilting her blouse. Thank goodness her jacket hid her nerves. "Excuse me, Mr. Nucretah," she squeaked.

"Rafe." He smiled.

The simple act of twisting up the corners of his mouth made her legs wobble. *Here's your chance, say something*. But she couldn't get out another word.

"A car will be sent for you at six tomorrow evening. Give Celeste your address before you leave." He leaned against his desk and stared at her. There was something unusual about the look, as if he were trying to see through her, but couldn't.

"But I..." mumbled Pepper, as the assistant moved to her side and indicated the door. "No." Pepper's heart raced and she took a step toward the Governor. She couldn't lose her chance. "I need to talk to you."

"Very well. We may as well talk now. Celeste, leave us."

The assistant pursed her thin lips and left them alone. Anxiety tightened Pepper's chest as she heard the door click shut. She needed information about her father and Nucretah's help, if he'd give it. Everyone knew the aliens were stubborn, controlling, unfeeling warriors. Sympathy wouldn't move him. But they had a clan mentality, and they valued family. Her father was all she had. Pressing that point might work.

"Be seated." He gestured toward one of the tufted leather chairs opposite him as he claimed his seat behind the desk.

How honest should I be? The man wasn't one to be played with, and rumors persisted of the alien's ability to read minds. She perched on the edge of the chair and clutched her computer to her chest. *Better to come out with it.* "First things first. I'm afraid I'm here under false pretenses. I'm Pepper Morgan and I didn't come for this. I just had to get in to see you." Waves of his displeasure flowed across the stone desk, rattling her.

His mouth tightened. "You may not have

intended to apply, but you've been chosen. My decision stands."

"What's the situation? Maybe we can work out a deal. You give me the help I need and I run your errands or whatever for a few days."

"It's nothing like that."

"What is it, then? I'm a hard worker. I'll do about anything for your help. It's important to me."

He stood and his mouth twitched. "Glad to know you'll make an effort. I've claimed you as my mate."

Her stomach plummeted, her legs shook, and if she'd thought running was an option, she would have. Her computer slipped from her hands and fell to the floor with a thud. "What? You can't. I can't. We just met."

"The binding is tomorrow night." He didn't bother to look at her and spoke into the intercom. "Celeste, get someone to escort Pepper home and pack her things."

She jumped to her feet. "No!"

"Not an option." He spared her a glance as he shuffled through papers on his desk.

'I won't do it."

"You will."

She slammed her hand on the desk and winced from the force. "But I don't love you."

"That's not my concern." He retrieved a page from the stack.

"It's not right. You can't mean to force me.

There are laws protecting humans from Kivronaian abuse." She rubbed the tender flesh of her bruised palm with her fingers.

He lifted his focus to her. The power and authority in his gaze made her squirm. This man held the lives of thousands in his grasp and she knew it. So did he. "Do I have to remind you that in this sector, I am the law?"

Though his voice remained soft, the harsh reality of that statement she knew too well. He controlled everything, from granting permission to leave Red Rock, to the blood tax on humanity. And now, he had his sights on her. "Why not claim one of the other women? I'm sure any of them would be ecstatic."

"I don't want any of them. I want you."

"Why?"

"You're different."

She quelled the urge to scream, her body as tight as a bowstring. "That's not much of a reason to get married."

"More than enough of a reason." The pronouncement was barely above a whisper, but it carried a lethal edge concealed in his velvet voice. "You said you'd do anything for my help. What do you want?"

"Want?"

"Yes. I tire of this argument and I've another meeting. Let's expedite this. We both know you must surrender."

She flinched. "You haven't given me much

choice."

"None." He put down the paper and moved close enough that she could catch his spicy scent, a mix of cinnamon and something unrecognizable that made her mouth water. His dark gaze leveled on her face. "I'm not negotiating. But I am willing to grant you a favor, call it a wedding present."

She looked him in the eye, trying to seem braver than she felt. "Do I have your promise?"

"Everything I say is a promise."

The chance of seeing her father had dropped into her lap, but at a high price, marriage to a cold, bloodthirsty alien. Fear clutched her heart. *I can do this. I have to.* She trembled as she forced out the words. "I'll agree and not fight you, but I want my father brought home."

He cocked his head and raised a dark brow. "A small request. Very well. Done."

Pepper released the breath she hadn't realized she'd been holding. Relief washed over her frayed nerves and tears filled her eyes. "Thank you," she murmured, staring at the carpet.

"Where might I find your sire? Is he in another sector or continent?"

She lifted her head and blinked back the moisture. "Kivron. He was transferred six months ago."

Rafe didn't move, didn't drop eye contact, but a shadow crossed between them. "I'll look into it."

Darkness invaded her heart and she feared. *I'm never going to see my father again.* "You promised." Her voice quavered as her emotions spilled over in silent tears. She hated that he saw her vulnerable.

His brown eyes softened and he placed his large hands on her shoulders, firm, but gentle. "I..." he hesitated. "I will keep my word."

Tremors ran through her body. His touch unnerved her. She needed to be held, needed strong arms to comfort her, a firm chest to lay her head upon, a safe place. She needed her father, not this stranger. Flashes of unknown need seared her, but they weren't hers. She shook her head, confused, and stepped back from his reach.

His mouth tightened, he put his hands behind his back, and stared ahead. "The binding will take place, make no mistake. There is no annulment and no divorce. It's eternal."

Her heart slammed against her ribs. "Eternal?"

"Due to the ritual's sacred nature, I can't explain what occurs. It's a simple ceremony. An appropriate gown will be provided."

"It's too fast." Panic raced through her veins. "Can't we wait a while?"

"To what purpose?"

"To get to know each other, of course." Her legs shook. She wiped her damp palms on the seams of her skirt.

"That's what the binding is for."

"You've got to be kidding."

He narrowed his eyes to hard, black slits of

determination. "I assure you, I'm not."

ABOUT THE AUTHOR

Sandy L. Rowland is an award-winning author who lives in the shadow of the Wasatch Mountains, and the twisted forms of the red desert with her loving husband and family.

She craves adventure.

Whether spending time in a sweat lodge in Southern Utah, living in a teepee for a month in New Mexico, or strolling the streets of Rome, she believes life is to be experienced.

You can learn more about Sandy and her books at: www.sandylrowland.weebly.com